Aimee Harvey is a disabled author and photographer with a dream. She always wanted to spread the word that it's okay to be different. And being part of the LGBT+ family is no different. Being part of the LGBT+ family herself, she noticed that there were not many books for the community, so she began writing. Aimee lives in the United Kingdom with her cat and is a university student studying photography.

Father Lexxie wishes to keep their life private, but they sure know how to spread the news of the LGBT+ community; collaborating with a good friend, Aimee Harvey, both together wrote a book about the LGBT+ community.

To my grandma,
'Well done, we are so proud of you… lots of love.'
You will always be missed.

Aimee Harvey

HOME

AUSTIN MACAULEY PUBLISHERS™

LONDON • CAMBRIDGE • NEW YORK • SHARJAH

A CIP catalogue record for this title is available from the British
Library.

ISBN 9781528950404 (Paperback)
ISBN 9781528972673 (ePub e-book)

www.austinmacauley.com

First Published (2020)
Austin Macauley Publishers Ltd
25 Canada Square
Canary Wharf
London
E14 5LQ

To my mum and my dad (oh, and my cat, Wolfie). Thank you so much for believing in me while writing this… it has been a long five years; all those trials that happened, such as my back problems with my health and putting up with my random moments asking what would be good for this or that and also the times I got really annoyed with the writer's block. And when I wouldn't do anything as I had an idea of what to write.

To my granddad. Even though you have dementia, I know you have still supported me, despite losing Grandma, you are doing so well and have supported me so much.

Jeremy Fielding, my old college mentor. Thank you for the guidance! Honestly, without a fellow writer, I don't think that this would have been good! If you want any ideas on what to write next, hit me up. I will help, haha! Also, thank you for helping me get through college! Honestly, if it wasn't for you, I think I would have dropped out in the first few months. Keep in touch!

Gerry Atkinson, hey girl. Thank you for helping me through the small time I had at university. Shame I had to leave! I will keep sending you little snippets of stuff I write and photos I take!

The girls in Morrison's cafe (aka Aunty Jeanette, Aunty Christine and Aunty Annette), thank you all. From the start to the finish, you have been nothing but supportive! Also, thank you for letting me put a small little bit in the book about you all! Thank you too for being there for Grandma… It's nice to know that someone was there for her when she was ill when I couldn't be there!

To my Grandma… You are gone but never forgotten, thank you for always being there for me and being there when I was struggling with life… Keep Sammy entertained and scamp up there… Love you and miss you.♥

Last but not least, the team at Austin Macauley. Without you, my publishing dreams would have never come true. You were the first lot I sent my book to and a straight acceptance! When I got the contract through, I just could not believe that my dreams were about to come true! Still cannot believe it!

Thank you all!
Lots of love
Aimee Harvey & Father Lexxie

Dear Diary,

Today, well, it wasn't a good day. I am only 12. No one should have to live the life I have. I do drugs and alcohol on a regular basis. Why, just WHY? I had a gig tonight, though Steyvan was next to me the whole time which was nice and sweet. But to make my day worse, I got kicked out of home. Not my fault I do drugs and alcohol. It's their fault. Now I live with Steyvan. A little backstory as this is my first entry.

I was forced alcohol when I was 5, drugs at 10 and had a son at 11. All by my ex foster parents. All will be explained properly soon, it's too emotional for me. Now, I am going to snuggle up to Steyvan. Yes, he's 16, judge all you want! He moved out his parents, found out what happened to me. He has a Shadow-branded piano. So I am going to wind down on that black beauty before a snuggle.

Gute Nacht

George.

Chapter 1

The thumping of my platform boots on the wooden floors as I stomped around gave me a fire in my heart. I was doing what I loved—performing. I did my normal long five-minute scream and looked up as I kept on screaming to see the whole of the Nautical-themed pub called Mariners in the seaside town of Ramsgate, Kent. It was full to the brim with fans. They all started singing along to one of the most popular song of ours—Screamo Choir.

'You're my desire, Screamo choir, my desire, Screamo choir.' They still carried on chanting that phrase while I did a "Screamo-rap" on top. 'I will never give you up, I know I've done that quite a lot, but my heart keeps beating, as long as I keep on cheating.' The song carried on right to the end and went straight into "The Smoke". 'You're just a little psycho, go find another Maiko,' I carried on to the very end, which was a lot quicker than I thought it would be. 'Your body they will be bringing, straight to the altar, with the revolver.' I dropped the mic and knelt down to the floor doing a loud scream as the band finishes up. I grabbed the golden specially made microphone and flicked my hair up so I was looking at the audience. 'Thank you for coming, people! See you next Sunday… You fuckers.' I looked around to see the rest of the band put their instruments down. 'Steyvan?'

'Yes, babe?' he said in his sexy, suave English accent while holding his hand out to help me up. I took his hand as he pulled me up with ease from the wooden floor.

'Go into my bag and grab my meds while I go to the bar and grab a drink for us all.' He nodded as I walked to the bar. 'Two Stellas, one orange juice and a gin and tonic and also a coke please. Not a line of it, dickhead.' The bartender nodded, getting ready to do our drinks and walked off as Steyvan returned.

'Here you go, sweetheart,' Steyvan said, giving me my medication box. 'G and T?' I nodded as I grabbed my orange juice to take my meds. 'Thanks, babe.' He took a sip and swallowed before smiling. 'You look beautiful.' He sat down and put his hand on my knee.

'Thanks… As do you.' I put my head on his shoulder and put a straw in my juice. 'Love you, Steyvan…'

'Love you too.'

'Hey, you gay boys!' We heard Ron, our drummer, shout. We sighed as I took my head off of his shoulder and he came up to us. 'So, I'm going to own my drink, go home and let you two shag!'

'Ron, will you just leave it that we're gay before I punch your fucking head in! That's immature and stupid to pick on people that are gay—accept it!' Steyvan said with annoyance in his voice. 'Anyways. You have to pack down. Cunt!' Steyvan turned away from Ron to accept the in-hand pay from the gig that we were promised. 'Thanks, mate.' Steyvan then turned to me for a kiss. 'I adore this nautical theme!'

'I do too! It's different…' We carried on talking in hope that Ron would go away. He eventually did. 'We best pack down, have we not? He won't do it!'

***

'I'll see you at home,' I said to Steyvan before kissing his gin-and-tonic-flavoured lips. 'I need to take a walk to clear my head. Kiss me again.' Steyvan smiled and kissed me again. 'Sorry… You know how much of a softie I am.'

'Yes. Yes, I do.' He held me in his well-sculpted arms as I put my head on his chest and we swayed side to side for five minutes. It was as if it was just me and him in the world. 'See you at home, sweetie.' He kissed me once, then twice then a small French kiss before leaving me with my guitar and violin.

'You are one lucky man, George.' The bartender said to me, smiling as he leant on the counter.

'I know I am… Anyways, I'm going for a walk.'

'Be careful, George. See you next week!'

'I will.' I grabbed my instruments and walked outside, where I lit a cigarette and then started to walk down the harbour.

***

On my way back, I saw a little girl lying in the doorway of the art gallery on York Street, whom I see every day. *Who is that girl?* I asked myself on my normal walk home from my gig I just did. Trench coat blowing in the wind and my makeup running down my face black and white streaks everywhere, and then the usual need to pee due to the cold gale blowing in my face and bare hands. The streets were dark, the streetlights did nothing really! But everything was the same. Down to the same little girl lying in a shop doorway just to stay out of nature's cold sharp bite that I saw every day, after every gig. I stopped and looked. *Do I wake her up? No, don't, George.* I said to myself, yet again, making a quick adjustment to the black guitar case on my back and carbon fibre violin case in my hand. I started to walk back home again. The cold nipping ever so slightly at my bare fingers. Yet the image of that little girl just lying there, with no covers or pillows, was still there. It was just a haunting apparition like always being visited by that one relative that had passed to make sure you are okay. 'I have to do something,' I said to myself, determined to help her. I rushed home and put my instruments down to ponder my actions with delicacy as I saw a note on the table from Steyvan.

Dear George
If I am not up by the time you get home, so very sorry, love.
Treatment is getting to me; I just need to rest.
Lots of many hugs and love

Steyvan xxx

That's fair enough, he needs the rest. I looked around the kitchen and spotted a flask. I then popped into the living room and my eyes spotted a plain white pillow and black fluffy blankets we never use, then a black big backpack which I never use. *I have just the idea!* I grabbed the blankets and pillows and the backpack as I grabbed some of my money off the piano too. I put the money in my coat pocket and put the pillow and blankets into the backpack. I quickly rushed into the kitchen and filled up the flask with hot chocolate and wrote Steyvan a note in case he woke up and I was not home.

Dear Steyvan
Popped out to see the girl that is on the streets. She's got no covers or anything.
I need to help her.
Lots of black lipstick kisses

George xxx

I put the flask and a few snacks in the backpack and put on my trench coat and gloves. *Take off your makeup, you knob. Don't want to scare her more than she already is!* I took off my makeup with a few coconut oil makeup wipes, put them in the bin and then made sure I have everything including my phone. *Let's go.*

I walked back down the cold harbour in the dark with my phone lighting my way. I walked down the street on the opposite side for better view as there was more light coming from a store. I saw the girl again. Lying in the same art gallery porch entrance and I then crossed over. I knelt gently beside her putting the backpack down as I carefully wiped her hair away from her face and noticed how badly greasy her hair was, then the smell. *I have to do something.* 'Excuse me?' I said softly. She woke up and clutched to her Peter Rabbit teddy and her small puppy toy for comfort with her eyes scared as anything. 'Hang on.' I put my hair up in a messy bun that held itself up. 'Is that a bit better? Haha, I'm George. George Grayham,' I said, trying to not come over as intimidating. 'I want to help you.' She relaxed as I grabbed the bag, I bought with me and bought out a blanket and pillow. 'I saw you had no covers and I thought you would like these.'

'Thank you, sir,' the sweet, timid as a mouse voice replied to me genuinely shocked. 'Why me?'

'I also bought you a drink of hot chocolate,' I said, pulling out the flask. 'And I see you when I come home from my gigs, I just know how you feel.' I come out while smiling. 'Do you want some food? I have money on me, so we can go get you something?'

'You have done so much already, sir, I can't accept that after all this. Thank you,' she said as her bright, brilliant blue eyes caught the light. 'Thank you.'

'Do you want to come home with me, to somewhere warm?' She shook her head. 'I'll come back tomorrow with more drink then, if you wish?' She smiled as her eyes lit up. 'If you ever see me wandering around, don't be afraid to come tap me on the shoulder, okay?' She hugged me as her fragile little arms wrap around me. I could feel she was stick thin. I was afraid to hug her in case I broke her.

'Thank you, sir, again,' she said, shaking. 'See you tomorrow.'

'You shall.' I let go of her and smiled. 'If you need me and I'm wandering around, honestly, ask me.' She nodded to me timidly and looked at the black blankets and the plain white pillow. 'What's your name anyway, I didn't catch it?'

'Breland. Breland Seppings,' she replied, smiling. 'Is this blanket and pillow and drink, for me?'

'It is. I hate seeing you here. I just needed to see if you were okay. I like your teddy and toy by the way!' I got £15 out of my pocket and gave it to her. 'Get yourself some hot food, okay?'

'I can't take that, sir,' she said, absolutely shocked.

'You will, okay?' She nodded and smiled and hugged me again. 'I will see you tomorrow and I might even join you, have a funny feeling my partners gonna kick me out any day,' I giggled, returned the hug and let go. 'Stay warm okay?' I said, shaking out the fluffy black blankets and plain pillow and wrapping her up in the blankets.

'Okay, and I like your accent. Where are you from?' she asked intrigued.

'Thank you and Berlin, Germany,' I replied, smiling and making my accent that slight bit thicker.

'I've always wanted to go there!' she smiled ear to ear.

'Maybe one day, I will take you. I'll tell you more about it tomorrow. Sleep well.'

'Good night,' she replied, lying back down, not letting her teddy and toy go.

**

I got back home and sat at the beautiful, black, full size, Shadow branded, specially made, Grand Piano in the modern living room, as I usually do to wind down. 'Babe?' I heard from behind me with a familiar male English accent. He sounded concerned.

'Hey, Steyvan. Sorry if I woke you up. You know that little girl that's homeless in town?' I said, hoping he doesn't change the subject.

'I do,' he padded along the fluffy rug in his bare feet to sit on the piano stool next to me, facing away from the elegant ivory keys. I looked at his bare chest and smiled. 'What about her?'

'Well, I just went to see her, and she's not doing that well,' I said, turning to look at him.

'Adopt her then,' he replied, smiling with a tired look.

'I can't. She doesn't want to leave.'

'Well. You know what to do, but come to bed, okay?' Steyvan said to me, getting up and padding back to the door. 'Or go get her now. If you want me to, I'll come?'

'I'll be up in a few. Just got to wind down.' Steyvan nodded and smiled. 'Night.' I turned back to the keys and started to play a classical piece called Thomhas Jayke I composed myself for a concert I did for Classical music. After a while, my brain finally relaxed enough for me to try drift off to sleep.

***

'You awake, babe?' I asked Steyvan, looking at him. He was snoring away. A leg and an arm hanging off the edge of the dark yet comfy bed. I smiled to myself as I pulled the blanket up to me so the cold breath of Mother Nature couldn't get me. I closed my eyes, but that was a mistake. All I saw was Breland, cold and shivering. But I couldn't wake up.

***

Dear Diary,

Steyvan, he's not well. I can tell that instantly. Just hope he will be okay. It's been over a year. He's the only one I've clicked with. BUT, in other news, I think I have managed to crack into the homeless girl's head. Her name is Breland. She's a sweetheart. Just hope she doesn't get hurt while I work on getting her into the house to be safe. Steyvan's on about getting a company up Grantham. I'm 13, not 16. Sadly. Just wait. My dad, well, biological one, has not even BOTHERED trying to get in touch with me. Oh well. My mother makes an attempt. Which, for me, is good enough.

Gute Nacht
George

***

Chapter 2

'No. Don't hurt me, I have children! DON'T HURT ME! PLEASE!' I yelled as I was crowded into a corner.

'George, YOU GOTHIC FAT FREAK. That girl, God. You fucking freak, who would help her?!' I threw a punch at the shadowed man.

'EAT THIS.' I yelled, running to Breland. 'Come with me. NOW.'

***

I bolted straight upright screaming not wanting to move. 'Whoa, George, you okay?!' I tried getting my breath back. 'Sweetheart, what's wrong?'

'Nothing. I–I'm fine.'

'No, you're not, sweetheart, what happened?' His concerned accent asked me.

'Just a nightmare. I'm fine.' I lay back down as I felt Steyvan's arm go around me. I put my hand on his and relaxed. My legs laced with his as I got comfy and snuggled up to him for warmth and comfort.

'It's okay, George. Don't worry, love. Go to sleep.' I felt him kiss my cheek, stroke my hair and relax while I silently close my eyes and went back to sleep.

***

Dear Diary

Another day, another gig. Not a good start to the day, but, it will do.

Later!

George

***

Chapter 3

I sat in Mariners before the gig with Andy, my manager, having a pint before I had to get ready. I grabbed my bag and laughed at what was in it. 'God, Steyvan! You know how to make me laugh.'

'What's that, mate?' I passed my bag to Andy, who looked in and saw a happy man wine stopper. 'That's cool. That's just brilliant!' Andy laughed and then laughed more. 'Not as funny as this,' the Scottish man said, pulling out something furry.

'Jesus, Steyvan. Yeah, he's getting none of that tonight,' I said, laughing and putting Andy's hand back into my bag to drop the tail. 'Shit! Better get ready.'

'You better!'

***

'We are The Deathbeds. If you are easily offended, well then.' I put my middle finger up as everyone said in unison— FUCK YOU! 'Get out if you are. *Danke.*'

***

'Stop playing,' I said to the boys. I looked past the crowd and out the door to see Breland smiling. I went outside and smiled. She looked at me as her face went to looking scared. 'Breland. It's me, don't worry, this is just my stage get up,' I smiled and hugged her. 'Come in.' I led her in and put a chair right next to the stage and she sat there. 'Back to it, boys.' The drums started up and guitar on the note it all paused on, like professionals so I could help that small homeless girl. 'You're just a little psycho.'

***

'That was brilliant, George, but why is your makeup like that?' I looked at her as she pointed to the mirror as a signal to look at my face. I looked at my makeup and it was white face powder with black lipstick and black eyes resembling a panda. 'I like it, but it's strange.'

'Stage makeup, miss,' Steyvan said, smiling bringing a pint of Stella Artois for me and an orange juice for Breland.

'Oh, hello… Thank you.'

'This is my partner, also known as Steyvan and he is the bassist.' He sat down as I kissed him and smiled. 'None tonight, babe. I saw what you put in my bag,' he giggled as Breland looked at me confused. 'You don't wanna know,' I smiled. 'Come home with us, okay?' She nodded and grabbed her bag as she downed the orange juice. 'Is the Lambo still out there?' Steyvan nodded. 'Good. You're driving, I've had too many. You're practically sober,' I said, keeping in a Buddy-The-Elf styled burp then letting it out. 'Pardon me.'

'What's sober?' Breland asked me, confused. *Turns out she's been on the streets longer than I thought.*

'Him. I'm basically tipsy. If you wanna see me drunk, come on a Friday night,' I laughed, handing Steyvan the car keys. 'Then I'll be drunk. Sober is basically where you've not had anything and are able to drive in a straight line. Unlike me so I'm being sensible as he's the designated driver anyways.'

'Oh,' she smiled, clutching her teddy, toy and a black backpack with the things I gave her.

'Let me finish this and then we'll go, okay? You are safe with us.'

'Okay. What do you sing? I've not heard it before.'

'Screamo,' I said before downing my pint. 'Ready?' I grabbed wipes out my bag as I got paid £300 in hand. 'Ooooh yeah, is next week booked, mate?' The bartender nodded and smiled. 'Awesome.' I wiped off all the black lipstick, white face powder and the eyeliner quickly and smiled. 'Back to normal. Usually, if I'm pissed that is, I can't take that off.' I chucked the wipe into the bin behind the bar and got up. 'And do that. Babe, remind me to take my painkillers when I get home. That five-minute screams killed me.'

'Okay, let's go.'

'Five MINUTES?!' Breland almost yelled in shock.

'World record holder in Germany for ten minutes, Breland,' Steyvan said to Breland, putting her bags in the car. She got into the car clutching her teddies.

'That is so cool!' I nodded as I got into the car, followed by Steyvan.

'Let's get home.'

***

We got home and I walked up the stairs to unlock the door. 'I might be drunk. Steyvan. Can you do it for me?' I giggled. 'Can't get the bloody key in.'

'That's what she said. Oh! Painkillers!' Steyvan said, opening the door with his keys.

'Oh, shut it. You okay there, Breland?' I asked her. She nodded as she grabbed and tugged my top as we all walked into the dark hallways. 'Get you in and up for a shower. You deserve one to warm up.'

'Thank you,' she said genuinely shocked and smiling. 'Is it okay if you can make me one of those hot drinks, the one you bought me? That was nice.'

'Sure! Jump in the shower and I will do.' Steyvan went upstairs while I went into the kitchen, turned on the light and poured myself some milk to try settle my stomach. 'Okay.' I got out a small black mug and put in four scoops of hot chocolate while waiting for the kettle to boil.

'You okay up there?' I yelled up while pouring the water onto the hot chocolate powder.

'Yeah!' Steyvan yelled back.

'Heya, Jacko, you okay, matey?' I said to an 18-year-old Jackson who just walked in, looking like she's just finished a gig. She looked at me smiling with a bright orange straw in her mouth. 'Want a drink to go with that straw?' She made a noise back as I got her out some orange juice. 'Take the straw out of your mouth, mate.'

'Sorry. I had a bit of a problem earlier and I've been refraining from abusing anyone. I may have a dick, but doesn't mean I'm male,' the Italian-accented Jacko said a little bit angry.

'Who said that, mate?!' I asked shocked.

'Some prick. "Oh you're not female, you are a wannabe female." MATE, if I was a fucking WANNABE female, I'd make the effort to look like a tramp, wouldn't I?' Her Italian accent rumbled out with frustration. Breland came down wearing a long top we had lying about and wet hair. 'Who the—?'

'You know that girl who WAS homeless, sis?' Jacko nodded. 'Her. Her name is Breland Seppings. That's that same girl.'

'WHAT!' I nodded. 'Hello! Nice to meet you! I'm Jackson.'

'Hello,' Breland smiled as her wet hair dripped over her face. 'Steyvan is very sweet, George.'

'That he is,' I said, smiling a certain smile while scratching my hair. 'Tomorrow, we will get you more clothes.' Steyvan came down with her other clothes and put them in the washing machine ready for a good wash. 'Then we will take you out and get you food and that I think.' I gave Breland her hot chocolate as Jacko sipped her orange juice through her "beloved" straw. 'This is the idiot to go to if you need anything to do with violins, that's a point, Jacko, got a spare G string?' I asked Jackson who was sipping a drink through her beloved straw.

'In my draws,' she said, winking.

'You know what I mean, you stupid bitch. Anyways. I'm gonna go wind down and I'll be hopping into bed once I'm calmed.' I walked through to the living room where sat the black grand piano with the elegant ivory keys. I sat down and stroked the keys and started playing some Beethoven and Bach with many more classical composers mixed in leaving everyone to go to bed.

**

I finally got into bed at 1 am ready to snuggle down in the nice satin bed sheets next to my loving partner. 'You awake, Steyvan?'

'Yeah. Why?' Steyvan asked me sitting up in bed.

'Just wondering.' I crawled into bed next to him and put my hand on his chest as my head snuggled into the crook of his neck. 'Love you.'

'Love you too, George. Night.'

**

Dear Diary

FINALLY! I got Breland somewhere warm and for a shower. About time too. Bless her, she needs a friend. I LOVE BEING 13!!! Got a gig at the O2 arena! But as I am writing this, I'm stoned. I've had 10 lines, a shot of jack and a bottle of brandy. My brain is 100%, officially, fucked. I feel sorry for my liver. But, again, NOT. MY. FAULT. Luckily, the contacts for my eyes I wear don't show how stoned and pissed I actually am. Time for bed I think. Read my mother's book she sent me, maybe scrapbook a little bit. No idea. I MAY just phone up Kaz. See how he is getting on with his dyslexia. Poor sod can't read or write! Let alone sign his own name. And he's a priest. What a combo. poor twat.

I'm going to take my stoner body to bed. 'Cause I feel like I'm dying of the munchies right now.
GUTE NACHT!

Georgie!

***

Chapter 4

'GOOD MORNING!' I heard a familiar German accent yell out. 'WHO IS UP, MY YUMMY BUNNIES?!'

'Oh God...' I said to myself as I lay in bed, covered in black satin sheets from my waist down. 'She's here. Okay.' I slowly got up and placed my feet in my slippers as I put my dressing gown around me making sure I had some form of underwear on. 'FUCK OFF, ODETTE!' I tied up the belt of my dressing gown as I walked out the room holding my head from the previous night.

'GEORGIEEEEE!!!!!!' I heard the accent yell up. I jogged down the stairs to see one of my two other triplet siblings here. 'How are you my sweet trippy bro?!'

'Considering you fucking woke me up, I'm fine.' I went to the counter and dragged out my skull cup from behind the kettle, put one spoon of coffee and two spoons of sugar in it and added some milk while waiting for the kettle to boil. I looked around the kitchen and at the clock to see it was 7 am as I put my hair up in a messy bun to keep my hair out of my face. 'You okay?'

'Hell yeah!' she said, kind of prolonging the word yeah. 'You?'

'I'm fine, just getting ready to wake up Breland and take her shopping for new clothes.' I looked at her face and clothing. 'You are too colourful and energetic for this time of morning... and for a person with a hangover.'

'Awh! Thank you! I come to see how Steyvan is getting on.'

'He's okay! Just tired as hell... Poor sod. How's the band going and your baby boy and your relationship with Mr

25

Moss?' I said, pouring the freshly boiled water onto a much-needed coffee.

'Oh, all that is fine! Jon is fine… But look at this rock,' Odette held her right hand out to reveal an engagement ring with one single diamond.

'OH. WOW. CONGRATS!!!!' I said, smiling hugely. 'OH MY GOD! DOES THAT CHANGE COLOUR IN THE LIGHT?!' She nodded. 'That's so cool! I'll let Steyvan wake up in his own time. I'll wake Breland up after a few sips of coffee so you can meet her.'

'Okay!' Odette smiled, cradling a Chameleon-shaped cup in her hands. 'I love this cup, it's too cute.'

'That it is!' I took a sip of my coffee and went to a black marble table and sat on a stool. 'All I have to do is sort out a few bits, then we are ready to tour.'

'Oh! Where you touring?' Odette asked me, baffled.

'Germany. The usual. Getting banned from like three to four arenas a year. Because of Heil Hitler.' Odette sniggered a little as did I. 'Best go wake up Breland.' I got up leaving my cup there just for now. I walked upstairs into the spare bedroom and smiled as I knelt down next to the bed to wake up Breland. 'Morning, sleepy head…' I said while nudging Breland. 'Time to wakey wakey… Someone downstairs wants to meet you.'

'George?' a sleepy Breland asked me. I nodded and smiled. 'Okay. I'll be down in a few…'

'Okay… See you in a minute.' I got up and smiled at her as she blinked her eyes open to focus on the room. I walked out and went back downstairs to find my puppy awake and ready to go. 'She's just waking up.'

'Okay.' Odette nodded. 'I don't know what to do…' she said with a tear rolling down her cheek along with a sudden change of mood.

'Oh, sweetheart!' I went up to her and took the cup out of her hands, put it on the side and hugged her. 'What's wrong?'

'I don't know.' I put her head to my chest and stroked her ribbon-clad, braided hair as I rocked back and forth to comfort her. 'I'm late, I'm so damn emotional… No idea what's happening…'

'Sweetheart… Come here, could you be, ya know…' She shook her head as I enquired as gently as I could. 'It then just might be all the stress of organising that world tour, sweetheart. Calm down, okay?' I rocked her a little bit as I carried on stroking her ribbon-clad braids. 'Calm…'

'I'm trying…' she sniffled as she took a few deep breaths. 'Sorry… I've been like this all week, bro…'

'It's fine… I've had days like this while organising,' I smiled as she calmed down. I held her at arm's length. 'Damn girl, what makeup did you use? It's not ran or anything!'

'It's a spray you put on. Like you and your Lipcote,' she smiled.

***

'Hello…' I heard Breland say after Odette fully calmed down.

'Hey, Breland. Hot Chocolate is on the side waiting for you.' Breland smiled then looked at Odette. 'This is my sister, Odette. She impersonates Boy George for a living.' Breland padded over to the counter quietly and shyly like a mouse grabbed the cup with hot chocolate in it.

'Hello…' Breland said after sitting down on a stool next to me.

'Hey. I'm Odette. One of three of that menace,' Odette smiled at me.

'Hey!' I said to her, looking sarcastically offended. Odette and Breland laughed.

'I'm gonna go get dressed, leave you two to chat and then I will be with you, okay? I shouldn't be long… Might even quickly braid my hair like yours, Odette.'

'See you in a moment!' Breland and Odette said as I padded up the stairs, just really hoping Steyvan was awake.

***

Dear Diary,

I am so damn fuckin' emotional. And stoned. Emotional and stoned. Not a good combo. My scleras are hiding my eyes luckily! Blacking out my eyes. If they weren't there, no idea what would happen!

Anyways, best get ready for the day! I will be back later!

George

***

A little note

I met Steyvan at a black-tie event. It was for musicians etc. and I was quite young. I saw him sat at the bar with a glass in his hand. Looking down. So I went up and said hi! It took me a LOT of courage to do, but I did it. Since then, we've been together since I was 12. He was 16 when he asked me... I said yes. I trained young as a priest... I'm going to skip to when I was 14. It will be easier. Now? Now, I'm a dead man walking...

***

Chapter 5

'On the road!' I started singing as I pulled out of the Moto services M2 in the UK in a black Lamborghini. Breland in the back, Steyvan next to me. I looked at the interior. Lovely black seats, not leather, and a lovely gothic like interior.

'Shut it, love,' Steyvan said to me prior giggling away to himself. 'Bless her,' he said, looking at Breland in the back seat.

'Not going to stop. Going to go straight there,' I said to Steyvan as I looked into the rear-view mirror to see Breland asleep. 'Bless her.' I turned my eyes onto the road and concentrated with all my might.

***

I applied the parking brake as Breland woke up. 'Welcome to Grantham.' I looked around Belton Lane and sighed. 'Best go find Mother, ain't we?' I lit up a cigarette before getting out of the car.

'George!' I heard a familiar Spanish accent say when I leant against the car.

'Talk of the devil.' I tapped the back-right door of the Lamborghini and smiled. 'Morning, Breland.' As I turned around, my long, blonde hair, big-boobed mother practically bear hugged me. 'Hi, Mother. Got a fag lit up, also, your boobs are strangling me,' I said, struggling to breath.

'Whoops! Sorry!' Mum said, backing away and holding me out at arm's length. I looked at her. A pin-up spider web dress with Victory Rolls in her hair that brought out her bright blue eyes and her slim figure with plain black heels. A priest with black and grey hair and facial hair also came out. 'KAZ!!

THEY ARE HERE!' Mum shouted with excitement. I took a puff of my cigarette and blew the smoke as Mum walked away and noticed Breland. 'Oh my Gosh! She is so CUTE!' she squealed with delight.

'Breland,' Steyvan said, letting her out. 'Come on, sweetie.' Breland got out as I put out my cigarette in a coffin-portable ashtray I pulled from my pocket.

'Is Siobhan and Dodi here?' I asked Kaz, concerned. 'And Odette with Johnny?'

'They are, mate!' Kaz said when he got to the car. 'Go inside duck… You need to rest in your condition.' His Lincolnshire accent flourished. 'They are in town, mate. They are all 'ere, George.'

'Good. How's your reading and writing coming along, Dad?' I asked Kaz as Mum sulked off, stopping halfway to take off her heels which showed her true 5-foot 3 height.

'Very well. Ta. I may 'ave to leave, early at about three, need to visit parishioners and that.' I nodded as I opened the boot. 'Holy Mary Mother of God. Movin' up 'ere, are ya?'

'No,' I said sarcastically. 'I'm just dropping off the problem child called Steyvan off.' I laughed as I saw Steyvan and Breland walk around the corner to the back door of the house. I and Kaz lifted the suitcases out of the car. A blue one, a black jewelled one and another plain small silver one. 'I bought my cassock and collar, so I'll join you for the parishioners if you wish?'

'Sure, mate! Do me a favour, or three actually. One: save me a fag. Two: don't let your mother lift anything. Her back is hurting and can't see her specialist. Three: get me alcohol. I bloody well deserve it. Also, a few bonus favours! Four: do this Sunday's sermon. I've been called up to Nottingham. Five: can you help me with reading and that and last but not least: put your hair up into a bun. When we go parishioner hunting that is.'

'Will do. Okay, I won't let her do that. I will, 'cause I want some too. I can do that, just tell me what to do. I can help you and I will as I need to wash it anyways. When will we stop at the church and that lot? Because I'm tired,' I said and asked, pulling up the handles on the suitcases to pull them. 'Is Br–Breland is awake.' I smiled as I saw her in the garden sniffing the flowers as I let out a little giggle and Mum sat there watching her through the window.

'We will go very soon. And thanks... Been trying to do paperwork and it's been stressing me out all day!' Kaz joined me taking the suitcases into a slightly old-fashioned, decorated house. 'Si and Dods are in town but should be back soon.'

'Okay. I have bought large print books, so we can work on them until they either turn up or we have to leave!' I put the suitcases down in a very small kitchen. 'Let's do this!'

***

I tied my hair up into a bun before putting on the long priest robe called a cassock and then followed by the collar to look presentable. I turned to Kaz who approved the look. 'Awesome! Let's go!' I put on my rosary as we said a little prayer.

'Ready! I'll see you later, Duck.' I looked over to see Kaz kiss Mum, who was lying on the sofa hugging her teddy. 'Love ya. Oh! Breland, I see you like Beatrix Potter! Garcia does too!'

'Love you too,' the Spanish accent replied.

'Let's go, George.' I walked out of the door as Kaz stepped out in his collar and black suit which was black smart trousers and a plain black smart button-up top with the priest collar. He let his black and grey hair stay down as it was only shoulder length. Mine, it was to the bottom of my back. 'Keep an eye on 'er, okay, Steyvan?' Steyvan nodded and smiled as Kaz closed the door and started walking.

'I was going to ask why you can't see her specialist,' I said to Kaz while walking down the street.

'He's got no appointments till next year. I even tried bribing the woman. Garcia is in a LOT of pain. I hate seeing it,' he sighed with a hint of sadness. 'It's getting to the point where some days she can't even move!' He smiled at me and chuckled, 'But she's doing well. Let's do this.'

'Don't tell me about your sex life… That's disturbing, that smile and chuckle when talking about Mum,' I said before laughing.

***

'You, my darling, have the charisma of a fucking cactus,' Mum pointed out to Kaz.

'Hey!' he yelled at her before bursting into laughter. 'So, Steyvan, ya popped the question yet?'

'I haven't, Kaz,' Steyvan's beautiful English accent rung out.

'You need to, mate. Bet he's gaggin' for a piece of you!' I looked at Kaz and laughed as cheeky smile played on his lips. 'Okay, bad priest, bad jokes, I know.' Kaz laughed again as he sat next to Mum. 'But I 'ave kiddys, a lovely wife and a loving family.'

'Your list of to do stuff is on the table. I'm popping out to meet George. Big George. I'm looking after him tonight and taking him home.'

'Okay, Duck. Gimme a kiss. I'll probably be asleep when you get back. Me legs are acting up.' I took off my cassock and collar and hung them up as Kaz and Mum kissed. 'Love ya, Duckie.'

'Love ya too. See you soon,' Mum said as Kaz got up and walked to the bedroom. 'Bless him.'

'What's up with him?' I asked Mum who was munching on a lemon and white chocolate muffin before she left.

'His legs are acting up. Sit with me, I have a few more minutes to go before I have to leave! Let's chill.'

***

Dear Diary.

I am so tired after that drive. So no long entry tonight! I'm going straight to bed.

Gute Nacht.
George.

***

Chapter 6

'So, what's for dinner?' I asked Mum as she stood in the church's kitchen grating two types of cheese.

'Your granddad is coming to cook cheese jacket potatoes! He should be here any minute now.' She grabbed some orangey-red cheese and grated that into a different pot. 'Red Leicester.'

'Ah.' Breland came in shy and scared. 'This is my mother, Garcia.' Breland hid behind me. 'Bless. Want a jacket potato that's lovely, crispy and loaded with cheese?' Her eyes lit up. 'Red Leicester or Cheddar?'

'What do they taste like?' Mum cut off a small bit off of each and gave them to Breland who tried them one at a time. First the Red Leicester, second the Cheddar. 'The red one is nice.'

'Sure thing! I can do that for you!' Mother smiled and turned to grate more Red Leicester cheese. 'Will she be okay around Dad?' My mother asked as Breland looked at me scared and hugged me.

'It's my granddad. World-known five-star chef! He's a brilliant cook. So, don't worry. Sweet as anything too! Is George coming around?' I asked Mum as she shook her head. 'Damn it! Breland loves the boy! She met Odette and was in love,' Mum giggled. 'Anyways, Breland, let's get you a new outfit.'

'Have fun!' Mum said, giggling as she turned back to what she was doing.

***

'So, let's see what we can find you. A dress, perhaps.' Breland looked at me scared. I looked around the vintage clothing shop with very little modern clothing. 'Just stick to me and you will be fine.' I grabbed a bronze basket as I walked over to a pink blossom dress. I picked up another one (one for Mum, one for Breland) and put them in the basket as her eyes lit up. 'I can tell you are in love. Let's see. Hmm. Blonde, blue eyes... Pin up I think! That and also a bit of modern.' I picked out a few dresses, jeans, tops and shoes for Breland to try on. 'Try these.' I looked in a mirror and saw behind me, my sister, Siobhan. A pink-haired version of me. Just brighter colours. 'Hey. Breland, wanna meet Siobhan?' She looked at me confused. 'HEY! GIRL G!' I yelled across the shop. Siobhan turned her head and walked over. 'This is Siobhan.' My sister smiled at Breland and Breland hid behind me.

'Hello...' Breland said shyly. She hid behind me with her arms holding clothes yet her eyes peeking out behind me.

'Hello, Breland. I'm Siobhan...' Siobhan smiled gently as Breland started to come out from behind me more. 'Don't worry. I don't bite.' Breland came out more and smiled coyly.

'Bless her. Wanna be a fashion adviser, Siobhan?'

'Girl, they will suit you, trust me!' Siobhan said in a slightly gay Brighton accent. 'Georgina is the best! Let me tell Dodi and I will help you. He'll go home.' I nodded as Siobhan ran over to her partner and then came back. 'Okay! Let's go!'

***

'So, now we've got you new outfits, let's try makeup,' Siobhan said, smiling with joy. 'Oh, neutrals. A pop of colour me thinks!'

'Makeup?' I nodded as Breland asked. 'I've never worn makeup.'

'We know the brands, don't worry, girl,' I said to a concerned Breland.

***

'Okay,' I said as we walked into a very busy Superdrug up to a brand called Makeup Revolution. 'Nudes, a bit of colour, red lipstick, a few nude lipsticks.' I looked to Siobhan for ideas. She had blue eyes, pink hair and a fair face. The makeup was bright yet simple. Liquid to matte lipstick in Regal, which had subtle hints of sexiness to it yet a side that says she's innocent, which, on Siobhan was always flawless, a pale eye shadow for base colour, a browny gold for crease with purple to add a bit of colour. The cheeks and face sculpting so subtle yet there. I could tell what palettes were used instantly.

'What does CF mean, George?' Breland asked me as I put my glasses on over my sclera-contacted eyes. 'Also, how long have your eyes been like that?'

'It means Cruelty Free and not that long, I put these contacts in before we left.' I picked up a 32-eye shadow palette called Mermaids Forever, a 12-colour palette eye shadows called Acid Brights and also a few more called Fortune Favours the Brave, Stripped & Bare, also a blush palette called Hot Spice. 'Si, is this the one you use?' She looked and nodded.

'Told you, you are in safe hands! Do you like the Gothic side of things?' Breland nodded slightly. 'Velvet black heart, Georgina too.'

'Okay, Breland. Let me borrow your hand.' Breland gave me her hand as I put up a Porcelain Soft Pink pressed powder by Makeup Revolution next to her hand. 'Yep! That is correct!' Breland smiled and shivered. 'Take my coat. It will keep you warm.' I took off my long coat and put it around Breland's shoulders.

'Thank you.'

'No problem,' I smiled quickly as my heart skipped a slight beat. *No. GEORGE NO! YOU ARE WITH SOMEONE ELSE!*

'You okay, George?' Siobhan asked me. I nodded as she put a sleek makeup travel brush kit in the basket.

'Okay. Kohl and Flick eyeliner. Sorted!' I got up as my hip clicked and I picked up the basket. 'Then we will pop into

Morrison's for a drink, okay?' Breland nodded and smiled. 'Let's go pay.'

***

'So, you ready to meet the family, Breland? And Grandad is lovely. Don't worry.'

'Okay,' Breland said to me shyly, holding a white full cup of hot chocolate. 'Who is he?'

'Big tits' father. Aka Garcia's father, George's granddad. Great cook, ex-saxophonist for Culture Club and shagging their backup singer,' Siobhan said to Breland, smiling innocently.

'What one?' I asked her. She looked at me with the *you-really-asking-me-that* look. 'Oh, yeah! Helen. She's working for the BBC now, ain't she? God no wonder Grandad's depressed. He ain't getting any nookie!' Siobhan looked at me almost spitting out her white Americano coffee with laughter.

'DUDE!' she said before trying not to cry with laughter as Breland sat there clueless. 'You don't wanna know!'

'Well. It's true,' I took a sip of my drink and laughed. 'And you really don't wanna know, Breland.'

'Okay, so, what do you do with all this? And who is Helen?' I opened my phone and went onto the gallery after putting a Superdrug bag onto the table.

'Helen is a vocalist and producer for the BBC producing the Brits,' I bought up a picture of a middle-aged, short, pale purple-haired woman and a middle-aged man with long brown hair together smiling and having a laugh. 'Helen and Tim.'

'Pretty.' I nodded and took out all the makeup out of the bag. 'So, what is all this?'

'Trust me, I do have a degree in makeup artistry!' I smiled and downed the rest of my drink. 'We have, about five eye shadow palettes, eye primer which is simple and easy to use. Pressed powder, but your skin is flawless, so you don't need foundation! Liquid lipsticks, which you cannot go wrong with. Hot Spice blush palette. Perfect Orange shade for your little 50s pin-up looks, but also, you have those pink shades for facial sculpting. But you do have a thing called strobing and contouring and a few more bits! So, you ready?' Breland shook her head and smiled then giggled. 'We will do it at home, don't worry!'

'Okay!' Breland drunk the rest of her drink and smiled. 'So, what is happening today?'

'Dinner, out to the gig,' I said to her downing the rest of my drink and looking out the window I saw a pale man with a bass guitar bag. 'AH-HA! I WILL BE RIGHT BACK.' I quickly took off my 5.5-inch Demonia platforms and ran between where we sat to outside. 'You got it?' He gave me the bass bag and opened it to reveal a red flying V distressed Shadow-branded bass. 'THIS IS BEAUTIFUL! Thanks, dude! You got the other stuff too?' He nodded simply as I got my wallet out and he handed me a bag. '*Danke*, Pedro.'

'Any time. Enjoy,' Pedro said gruffly, taking the money and walking away.

'Oh, I will!' I walked back in with the bass on my back and bag in my hand. 'Hehe!' I giggled like a little kid on Christmas getting their red bike they always wanted. I sat back down smiling.

'What's up with you?' Siobhan asked me, giggling. 'And what have you got?'

'Nothing,' I said quickly and bluntly letting my German accent tease her.

'Oh! I know what it is!' she pointed to Steyvan who was just walking to the table. I nodded and smiled quickly before he could catch on. 'Ohhh, okay.'

'Yeah. Shut it, Siobhan,' I said, laughing. 'Hey, sweetheart,' I said to Steyvan as he sat down. I kissed him and smiled, then got my platforms on. 'You okay?'

'Yeah… Just a headache. You?' he asked me grabbing his medication.

'Knackered. How's the spawn of Stan?'

'Fucking Stan?! You're a Goth! Not a poof!' Siobhan said, confused.

'They are fine, honey, and he calls Satan Stan for some odd reason.' Steyvan chuckled with a grin on his face. 'George, are you stoned?' Steyvan asked, looking at my eyes.

'I maybe. Why?' I asked, looking at him worried. 'It's just my meds.'

'The new ones?' I nodded, smiling. 'Ah, okay. Just wondering. Don't go back to drugs please, my dear love.'

'I won't, Steyvan….' My heart sank as I said that. *What he doesn't know can't hurt him…* I thought to myself. *Or can it? Stop it, George. If he doesn't know, it can't hurt him majorly. STOP NOW.*

'George, you all right?' Steyvan asked me a bit worried. I nodded to reassure him that I was okay. 'Want to talk, sweetheart?'

'No… No. It's just the tour getting to me. That's all.' I saw Breland looking at me worried. 'I'm fine, Breland… My happy pills ain't working! You seen Dad?' Steyvan shook his head as he put his arm around me.

'No, he's at work. Siobhan, can I have a sip please?' She nodded as Steyvan took a sip. 'Thanks. How can you drink that? It's more sugar and milk than coffee!'

'I'm not sweet enough and my sugar was low, go shag a pig, Steyvan.' She had a giggle after she said that. Proud of herself for such a quick comeback.

'If I wanted my comeback like that, I would—nope. Not going there.' I started laughing halfway through Steyvan saying that. 'You okay?'

'Pervert.' I nodded as I tried to stop laughing. 'Georgina, calm your tits,' Siobhan started telling me as I laughed a little more. 'He's okay, Breland. Just tired I think. Tired and very giggly as his MEDICATION IS RUNNING OUT!' I snort-laughed a little before trying to calm down.

'It's not, it's just he reminded me of something that happened,' I said, slightly calming. 'You really don't wanna know!'

'Okay.'

'Let's go back before I die of laughter and people look at me. They are already looking at me because of how I look,' I said, trying to stifle more laughter.

'Calm. Where's Kaz?' Steyvan said to me smiling, trying to hold in laughter.

'Parishioner hunting, as he calls it.' I put on my trench coat and did up the nine buttons quickly after putting on my boots again. 'Come on, Si, let's go and get Breland and I sorted. Breland, do you play any instruments?'

'Yes, Violin,' she said, smiling.

'Oh! Might have a job for you! Depends how quick you can learn it.' I heard a bang and looked. 'Oh God. I'll be back.' I ran over to see a woman just coming back from being unconscious. 'Whoa, you okay? CAN WE HAVE SOME HELP HERE?!' I yelled, hoping someone would come over to help. 'It's okay, I am trained,' I said as the young woman came around. 'Do you have ID and someone for me to ring?' She pointed to her bag. 'In your purse?' She nodded as much as she could as I grabbed her bag and went into her purse. 'You okay? Just keep talking if you can?' I looked at her ID. 'When did you last have insulin? I see you are diabetic.'

'This morning.' I just about heard what Clara said, luckily I could lip read or that could have gone wrong.

'Okay, I'm going to do another one for you in your leg, okay?' I rolled up her leggings as far as I could before grabbing her insulin injection. 'Ready?' I did it for her quick and easily. 'Take your time in moving, I have time, okay?'

'Thank you.' I helped her sit up and put her purse and ID back into her bag.

'Look, it's no problem.'

'You're George Grayham, of that band, The Deathbeds?'

'Yes. I am also trained medic. And diabetic myself. Jack of all trades, master of none.' I put my arm under her as she tried to get up to sit on a chair. I slowly guided her down to sit. I went into my pocket and gave her a backstage pass to the show tonight. 'Come along,' I smiled as she mouthed *Thank you* to me. 'No problem. Want me to stay for a little longer to make sure you're okay?'

'Please.' Steyvan, Breland and Siobhan walked over with my stuff to make sure I'm okay. 'Thank you, George. I'm Cora. Cora Ash.'

'Like Downton Abbey, Cora?' She nodded slightly. 'This is my boyfriend, Steyvan, my sister, Siobhan and my best friend, Breland.' They all smiled and sat down as people crowded the area.

'Hello. I'll think I'll be okay now, George, Ta. But can I have help getting up?' I got up and helped Cora get up and in a comfy position for her by piling her coat on her chair. I sat her down again, slowly but surely. 'Ta… I'll see you tonight?'

'You sure you are okay?' She nodded, smiling. 'Okay. That also gets you into rehearsals 6 pm and that will get you into soundcheck too. Come along.'

'Thank you,' she said, shocked.

'I'll see you soon,' I said, smiling sweetly. I got up and grabbed my stuff as Cora started to talk to someone else. I sighed and walked away with the bass on my back and my bag in my hand.

'You okay, Georgie?' Siobhan asked me as I nodded. 'Let's get you fed, because I don't know about that Cora needing insulin, I think you need it!'

***

Dear Diary
I am stoned to hell. Just… Absolutely stoned…
Let's do this gig.

Georgie.

***

Chapter 7

'Is that better?' Siobhan asked me after injecting insulin into my leg. 'You look it!' I nodded and smiled. 'Okay, want some food?'

'Please. An apple,' I said, grabbing my makeup bag. 'Shall I go metal or just pure full out Goth?'

'GOTH!' Siobhan said, laughing. 'Here's your apple, lady muck.' Siobhan chucked an apple at me and I caught it with ease. 'What time are you leaving?'

'I'm thinking 4. Then I can get ready, set up gear and then make sure it's all okay, rehearse etc. You opening for us?' I conversed to Siobhan.

'I am! I'll do, Girl George. Is it cool if Greg can come around?'

'That's fine! Greg's a nice man,' I said to her munching on the apple. 'Should I use my platforms?' Siobhan thought for a small moment and then nodded. I looked at my phone and saw a text from Steyvan. *Hey sweetheart, I have something for you. I will see you soon. Love you!* 'Aw! Bless him! Love him to bits.'

'I thought you did,' Siobhan said with a giggle. 'Think he'll pop the question?'

'Nah, we said just stay partners. We get shit for being gay as it is,' I said, sighing.

'I used to be lesbian and got engaged. I got shit but ignored it! Best you get ready as have I. Go on then, you clodhopper.' Siobhan grabbed her own makeup bag and opened it as makeup fell out of her bag. 'I need a bigger bag.'

'You do!' I sat up on the big black, full length, luscious sofa. 'I don't!' I reached back behind me and bought out a black aluminium beauty case with all my makeup in. 'You need one of these. OKAY. SKIN CLING! WORK YOUR MAGIC!'

***

'Are the Shadow 57's set up?' I asked Tom, the sound engineer.

'Yep! They are just being turned on. Shadow Vox 10 is up and on, Shadow FOH's and that are up, 60 Shadow amps are out. Everything is sorted and yes. That bass is out,' he said to me, smiling. 'Is there anything else?'

'Awesome, mate! Is there anything else that needs to go out? The drums are all set up etc. as I can see, so, that's cool.' I looked at the full Shadow-branded setup and smiled. 'We have people coming to rehearsals today. Just people to watch and that lot! Is the live feed set up?'

'That it is, all set up and ready to go,' he flicked on the projector and I stepped back into the huge Nottingham Motorpoint Arena. He picked up a walkie-talkie and turned it on. 'Mate, dance about in the dressing room please.' All of a sudden, the dressing room was on the screen and a small woman with makeup in her hands came on the screen dancing around. 'There you go! And it is smash proof, so you can do your usual.'

'That's good,' I smiled as I looked around the 10,000-capacity arena. 'This will be the best show I think in ages.' The stage was huge, seating well organised, then a lot of room for mosh pits and the Wall of Death to happen.

'So do I!' Steyvan said, smiling. 'Thank you for the bass! It's lovely!' I heard come from behind me.

'No problem, love. Saw it and I knew you would love it.' I turned around to put my arms around his neck and kissed him. 'What's up?'

'Nothing why? Just the pain, the usual,' Steyvan said, smiling. He put his arms around my waist and put his forehead on mine. 'Just. Don't fuck yourself up, okay?'

'I won't. You be careful yourself,' I said to him, letting my nose touch his. 'Eskimos kiss like this,' I laughed as he bear-hugged me as a small joke. 'Anyways, best get ready for rehearsals.'

'Yes. I love you. How many VIP's for rehearsals?' Steyvan asked me, letting his lips touch mine.

'Not too sure. Not too many I hope, you know how I—' He kissed me and chuckled. 'I, um, get, I should babble more often,' I said, crossing my legs and doing my coat up.

'Now, get your butt into the dressing room, get ready for rehearsals, pee or whatever you do and then rehearse.'

***

'Okay, let's rehearse!' I said as people came in. I had scleras in that blacked out all my eyeball. No makeup, but it would do. 'Heya, everyone!' My eyes laid on Cora. She wore a black small dress, Black ripped tights and some black high heel boots with a few accessories that just made everything come together. *She's beautiful. Nope, George, STOP!* 'How's everyone?'

'I'm fine now. Thanks, George,' Cora piped up shyly.

'No problem. Now. You will see us, in our height of stupidity, our height of annoyance and our really weird antics on stage during rehearsals. I'm very sorry for my face, and what you are witnessing, 'cause I look like a tramp on crack cocaine currently. So, let the weirdness COMMENCE!'

***

'So, what's this?' someone from the group asked, pointing to my earpiece.

'It's so I can hear myself singing, the drums etc. and so I don't need to worry and if say, my mic goes, I can also hear Steyvan's, so I can use whatever one I hear, also it helps me with click tracks of say, The Smoke. It's a helper. It also helps me with the set list, because I become slightly dyslexic on stage,' I said slightly embarrassed.

'That's so weird. What makes you dyslexic on stage then? I never knew that,' Steyvan said to me.

'The lights. 'Cause of how it flashes etc. it makes everything arse over tit for me.'

'Ah, okay. Any other questions?'

'Why are you all so hot?' Cora asked. I laughed as I pointed to Steyvan.

''Cause we can be.' Noises under the stage started happening which made us all look behind us. 'What the—?'

'That's what I'm thinking.' A hole caved in on the stage. 'WHAT THE—?!' A head popped up and laughed. 'DUDE, WHAT?!'

'Stage riser. Had a bit of problem with it. Sorry! Shoulda warned you!' The head went back down as I shook my head.

'*Danke*,' I said sarcastically. I looked around the arena and smiled. 'Well, time for backstage, you all join us to get ready and, um, well, yeah! Let's go!'

***

'THERE'S A 'OLE IN MY 'ULAROOP.' I heard coming from a dressing room after the VIP experience finished. It repeated. And repeated. And repeated. And repeated.

'What the fuck?' I said to myself. 'Just. What?' I laughed. I looked in a room that had *Kazarian Smith* on a "plaque". I opened the door to see my mother's partner doing the exercises. 'DAD?! WHAT THE FUCK?!'

'Stampy, blame your father.' He picked up a pair of heels and smiled. 'Don't tell your mother.'

'I saw nothing.' I leaned against the doorframe as he also grabbed a dress and hung it up. 'What the hell?'

'It's a long story, I've not been. Myself. When your mother goes out, I just dress up as old me. And that's happening tonight.' He grabbed a ukulele and a guitar. 'She doesn't know, okay?'

'I never knew you were female; it was a surprise! Be yourself.' I said to Kaz supportively.

'I was. It was a horrid time in my life. But now look at me. Living my life!'

'You are doing so well, Dad. Don't give up and beat that anorexia. You are better than it and look beautiful and handsome however you look. If you need me, I'm over the way, okay?' He nodded as he started tuning his guitar. 'Want a hug? You look sad.'

'Please. I'm not sad, just sad that I can't express myself like how you now know.' I hugged him and smiled when we broke the hug.

'Be yourself around me all you want, there is no harm in that, Dad. I'll be back in a few to check on you. You playing with the band tonight, ain't you?' He nodded as I walked back to the door of my dressing room, leaving his open. 'Okay, I'll come to get you! I'll do your face too if you want me too? Make you look like old you if you show me a picture?'

'I'd love that. Thank you, George.'

'No problem.'

***

'So, You all ready?' The band nodded as I looked at the door. 'This is Arianna Smith. Formally Kazarian to us.' Everyone gasped simultaneously.

'Hey, guys,' Kaz said in a way that his voice was female.

'Yes, it's gonna be good for him. Grab your guitar and Uke and we will take the piss out of support.' Kaz ran in his heels, black tights and Black long Victorian-style dress to grab his guitar and ukulele as I got on a bright pink wig. 'What?! If I'm gonna take this piss out of support, gotta play the part!'

'That you do!' I laughed and smiled. 'So, You ready?!' Steyvan turned on the camera and I grabbed a microphone and smiled. I had a live feed from the stage so no problem. I started pretending to be Siobhan for a laugh and everyone played up behind me pretending to be the band.

***

The fun carried on for an hour while Siobhan played as support. Not very metal, but it'll do! I finished off my makeup while live feed was still going. 'See you fuckers in a moment,' I said in my stage voice, grabbing the camera. I walked over to the fake mirror and lobbed the camera screaming as loud as I can which sent a "dead" signal to the crowd. I walked under the stage to the stage riser and crouched down with my platforms, black clothes and full on white face, black lips and panda eyes with the Shadow Gold Vox mic in my hand. 'Let's do this.'

**

'Guys,' Steyvan said, stopping the crowd. It was a sold-out show! He took off his new red Flying V bass and put it on the stand next to him. 'Um, this is awkward,' he said then grabbing his mic off the stand. I looked at him confused. 'Well, for a while, me and George have been going out. This sclera beauty has been mine for over 6 years.'

'HA GAYYYY!' our drummer, Ron, yelled.

'Go fuck yourself, Ron. Go fuck yourself. Anyways. As I was saying. That Sclera beauty has been mine for over 6 years. I wanna change that.'

'Steyvan, what?' I said with the mic to my side. I put my hand over my mouth in shock.

'George Lunar Grayham,' Steyvan got out a box from his pocket and opened it as he got down on one knee as I started crying with my hand still over my mouth. 'Will you be mine… but for life?'

**

Dear Diary

HE PROPOSED!!! On stage in front of all those people! I said yes! I'm only 14.

God too much excitement for me to handle!!!!!

I'm going to go and relax 'cause I'm too happy. Too happy to do anything. So I'm going to try and wind down... if I can. Steyvan's asleep and resting up. His treatments finished and got the all clear. Which I love.

Gute nacht
George

***

Chapter 8

'Tim, stop,' I heard my grandma say as I also heard saxophone playing *Pennsylvania 6-5000* by Glenn Miller. 'Tim. I swear. Carry on, that sax will be so far up your ass, you will be able to PLAY with it.'

'*Pennsylvania 6-5000!*' I heard an English posh cockney accent say before saxophone starting up again.

'I fucking swear, Timothy. STOP!' Grandma's English accent said, slightly annoyed. 'I may have been able to put up with it in the Culture Club days, but not now, stop!'

'Okay…' I heard my granddad reply to her sounding like he's done something wrong. 'Best get on with dinner though!' I looked through the door or the kitchen and saw Grandad put his arms around Grandma while laughing. He rested his head on top of hers and smiled, 'So what's happening now?'

'You cooking. That's what is happening,' Grandma said, moving from Grandad's grip to wander around the kitchen.

'Grandma, can I talk to you please?' I asked her, worried.

'Sure! Gimme a sec, Tim. I will be back.'

'That's what I was afraid of,' I heard my granddad say as I laughed as Grandma walked towards me. The heavy set, short and purple-haired grandma of mine walked out to where I was in the hallway and leaned against the wall.

'What's up, Georgie?'

'The sky,' I replied with a slight chuckle. 'In all seriousness, I don't want anyone to know but I trust you. It might be easier if I show you.' I walked to the bathroom and got in front of the huge lit-up mirror. I grabbed my Sclera contact lens case and took the black-out lenses out. I blinked a few times and turned to Grandma. 'I'm stoned to hell. Steyvan doesn't know.'

'You should've told me earlier, sweetheart. But why the drugs specifically? Coping mechanism?' I nodded and sighed. 'Look. If you need to rant or anything, you can come to me.' She put her arms around me as I stopped myself from crying. 'It's fine to struggle. But please don't do drugs. Does your mum and dad know?' I shook my head once and turned around to the mirror to start doing makeup on one eye. 'Okay, well. We will get through this together.'

'Okay. Thanks. I knew you'd be the best to go to. *Danke*.'

'No problem, sweetheart. Want me to stay with you? I know some tricks to de-stone you quicker?' I nodded. 'Okay. What do you think of this?' I turned around to reveal a smokey-eye look on my right eye. 'Love it! What's happening?'

'A gig.' Grandma just looked at me with the awesome look she usually has. 'Yeah. Classical. Don't want to do this.'

'Want a singer?'

'Know the lyrics?'

Grandmother nodded and smiled.

'Awesome. You are in.'

'Awesome! I'll go get ready. What should I wear?'

'Smart and that. I'm in a suit for tonight's gig.' She nodded and walked out as I took a deep breath. 'Okay. Keep a calm, cool and level head, George.'

***

'You ready?' my grandma asked me as I nodded, breathing heavily to calm myself down. 'Go on. Go get 'em with Thomhas Jayke.'

***

'Thank you for everyone that came out today for this classical concert. It was for my late son, Thomhas Jayke. All proceeds will go to the hospital that helped and charities. Thank you.' I looked over to my grandma who couldn't stop smiling. *You did it!* she mouthed to me.

'I… Steyvan! What?!' I said to him in shock as he stood there looking at me in the dressing room.

'Yeah,' Steyvan simply replied with a smile.

'What? You're saying I can get pregnant?' Steyvan nodded as I sat down in shock.

'Well, we knew that you were a working hermaphrodite. But, of course, we did keep that a secret… it's a working womb.' Steyvan replied confused.

'Yes… Want to try?' I said to Steyvan still in shock.

Steyvan looked at me with a very confused yet straight face, then all of a sudden, a big smile appeared and he shouted those 5 words; 'When can we get started?!'

***

Dear Diary.
I CAN GET PREGNANT!
That is all.

Gute Nacht
George xx

***

Chapter 9

'Not this time…' I said to Steyvan who sighed. 'But it's worth trying!' I said to Steyvan as he looked up at me and smiled. 'What's up?'

'Got a huge building.' I looked at him confused. 'You know my company?' I nodded as I sat down next to my beautiful blonde partner. 'Well, we are expanding Mr Vaughn-Ray! Would you like to be a co-owner? You are classed as a Vaughn-Ray my soon-to-be hubby… It is called Vaughn-Ray LTD after all!'

'I'd love that!' I said happy as I hugged Steyvan and kissed him.

'You can have a recording studio too!'

'Let's do this, *meine leibe*!'

***

Dear Diary
WHAT IS STEYVAN THINKING?!
Oh well. His fault!
I'm going to go and sort out everything. Unpack all our goodies etc.

Gute Nacht
George xx

***

Chapter 10

I stood in the huge warehouse of Vaughn-Ray LTD with my 3-year-old daughter and my eldest son was elsewhere as my drummer walked up to me. Ron wore a long coat to keep him warm. 'How is the family?!'

'Fine! Scar is still there!'

'So when is the band starting back up, Anolin?!' Ron asked, intrigued. My stage name is Anolin.

'When I'm feeling better, Ron. My body is fucked to say the least.' I looked over to see Steyvan bringing in a female brunette client. Japanese looks yet a beautiful floral dress on. 15 years old. Blonde hair with a scared look on her face. 'Hello! Welcome to Vaughn-Ray LTD! I am George Vaughn-Ray!'

'This is Bethan. Drugs case. Mainly cocaine aka bath salts. So she has come for a live-in help... Bless her! Though she may seem very shy and fragile and honestly, she will get upset at the flip of a coin, but, by heck if you get on the wrong side of her, you will know about it very very quickly.' Steyvan said to me while guiding Bethan in. I nodded and kept smiling to look friendly. 'Come on, Miss Millie-May! I will show you around!' Steyvan said to the client. He walked off talking to her looking like a right professional.

'God, what I would do to that ass. Oh. Wait. I already do.'

***

I was doing my normal routine, locking up the building and checking around the rooms to make sure everyone was okay. Until I came to room 4. Bethan's room. I heard a small crying sound, just like if someone was trying to muffle their screams and cries for help. I knocked on the door and she went quiet. 'It's George. Can I come in, Bethan?' She made a small noise as if to say yes. I slowly opened the door with my keycard and poked my head around. I didn't have Johnny with me, so I was okay to do what I wanted! 'You okay? I was just doing my rounds and heard you crying?'

'I'm. Just lonely.' I sat down on the bed next to her and hugged her. 'You look nice.'

'As do you. I'm here, okay?' I smiled and broke the hug. 'You are not alone, you are not on your own, if you ever need me, just let the reception know and I'll come and see you.'

'Okay. Thank you. Thank you so much, George.' The brunette-haired, tanned-skin woman said as my partner poked his head in. 'Babe, Breland is here to say goodbye.'

'I can't do goodbyes, Steyvan,' I said to my partner as he poked his head in the door. 'Tell her. She's welcome here anytime.'

'I will do,' Steyvan said to me leaving the room then popping back in. 'In fact, I will make her stay. It's too dangerous for her to be out there. Is there any room available?'

'Well, yeah. All of them apart from this one! Put her in room one! She'll be comfy in there.'

'Okay.'

The door closed as I looked at Bethan in the eyes.

'Thank you again, George. Your company here, everyone is so sweet and helpful. I wish I've heard of this company before. I've seen you live a few times. I love the band,' Bethan said to me in a small sweet Japanese accent but very fluent English.

'Any time. Anyways, I should go and let you get sleep. Goodnight. If you need me, I'll be in my office, okay?'

'Okay, thank you,' Bethan said, hugging me one more time.

'Good night, Bethan…'

'Good night.' I got up and left her room and closed the door.

'Good morning, sweetheart…' I heard from Steyvan as I sat in our office at my desk looking at the wedding photo. *Damn… A year tomorrow, I'm one, damn lucky man…*

'You okay?'

'I'm fine, Steyvan… What about you?' He put his arms around my neck and draped them down my chest. 'I'm fine, thank you… So, what's on the agenda for today for the group?' He lightly placed his chin on my head and looked at my screen. 'Uhhh… Let me look.' I typed into the computer the date. 'Twenty-fifth of the first two-thousand-and-thirteen… Um… A-ha!' I scrolled down and found the events of the day. 'Today is just getting to know people really. Lunch at 12pm and then dinner at 5pm.' Steyvan kissed my head and then stopped hugging me. He went over to his desk and smiled. 'Oh… first anniversary tomorrow!'

'That it is! What do you want to do?' his seductive English accent asked me. 'Spend the day together… Maybe, have some fun.'

'That can happen…' Steyvan said to me, looking at me with a seductive look in his eyes. 'Or it can happen now?'

***

Dear Diary

I love him too much… we zinged…
I'll be back soon.
Auf Wiedersehen

George

***

The Wedding Day

I woke up, shaking, withdrawal symptoms kicking in. 'Nope. Not today.' I sat up to see Leeds Castle, where I was getting married. 'These shakes are just nerves, George.' I sat up in the silk bedding, making sure I had underwear on. 'Good... At least that is one thing I do not have to worry about...' I uncovered myself to go to the bathroom as I heard a small knock at the door, then a piece of paper being shoved under it. I put my feet on the floor firmly and looked. I recognised the handwriting. 'Steyvan...' I got up and held the letter. I then opened it carefully to have a read:

Dear George.

Thought I'd say that I love you.
I will see you at the altar later today
Lots of Love

Steyvan
XXX

'Oh... Steyvan...' I sniffled slightly before smiling. 'Thank you...' I sighed happily and put the letter on the bed. I shuffled to the bathroom and looked in the ornate mirror. 'What?' I touched my face, like it was the first time I ever saw myself. 'This sober thing is weird.'

'We are here for the groom!' I heard a familiar French accent yell out as the door opened. 'Hey, George!' I looked out of the bathroom as Marilyn stood there, in a black suit, blonde hair looking presentable, while in shock. 'Shit! Are you sober?! What even?'

'Forget that, Maz. How's Steyvan?' I asked as a female walked in before shutting the door behind her.

'Nervous, but fine. I am so proud, George!' Marilyn hugged me as the female sat down. 'Right. Do your teeth, then come out. I have someone to take you through things.'

'But I'm already out! I'm gay!' I laughed quick as no one else found that good. 'Okay, okay. I'll go do my teeth and that.'

***

'So, this is Wolfie! She is a hairdresser, MUA and photographer. BUT she does work here.'

'Um… Hi,' I said very awkwardly. 'May I just ask, why is your name Wolfie?'

'After a cat that barks… My cat thinks he's a dog…' she said with a full American accent as I grabbed my suit out of the wardrobe with my platforms. She wore a smart skirt suit in black and white, with vintage line nylon tights and vintage black suede kitten heels. 'You will be fine. The staff here have worked so hard on this wedding.' I got out my lip scrub and applied a decent amount before vigorously rubbing it in, then licking it off. 'Want any help?'

'Nah, I'm good, thanks though.' I grabbed my liquid lipstick in black, eyeliner and mascara, then done my insulin by jabbing myself in the leg.

'My brother's diabetic,' Wolfie said to me. 'What type are you?'

'Type one,' I replied with a smile, while disposing the used needle properly.

'Ashleia is too!' I turned to her and gave her a look. 'What?'

'Ashleia Peabody?' Wolfie looked at me before running her hand through her black shoulder-length hair, then nodded.

'I know him! I know your daughter too! Olivia.'

'How do you know them?' she asked, pleasantly surprised.

'They played a gig at the company once.' She smiled and laughed slightly. 'They are really good! And your daughter is pretty cute.' I got my hair spray and styled my mid-back black hair to a nice style that would not get in my way.

'Well, thank you! And they are good!' she smiled again, but a bigger smile. 'Want a tip?'

'Yeah. I have not done this before.'

'Smokey eyes. Catch your hubby's attention. Also with those blue beauties, they will just pop like a balloon!' I looked at her confused. 'It's a saying… okay, pop like colour underneath a shit tone of black.' I breathed a slight sigh of relief as I looked at my hands, which were still shaking slightly. 'You okay?'

'Withdrawal. I'm fine.' Marilyn looked at me concerned. 'NO! I am NOT having any drugs today. No.'

'May I ask what you take, sir?' Wolfie asked, intrigued.

'Call me George, Wolfie…'

'Anything he can get his hands on, girl.' I rubbed my face with my shaking hands, in hope that it would calm me down. 'You sure you are okay?' I nodded. 'Okay, well, it is time to get dressed.' Wolfie got up and grabbed my suit and smiled.

'I'll help you, George.'

I nodded.

'Maz… I am slowly but surely getting there.'

***

All suited and booted and ready to go, my grandfather walked in. 'Hey, George… you ready?' I nodded. 'Maz told me… I am so proud of you, mate… Sober and clean for the day! Give us a hug.' I hugged the tall man I call my grandfather who was wearing a black suit and a white rose on his lapel. When we broke the hug, I looked behind him to see Breland poking her head around.

'Hi, George…' she poked her head around even more to reveal bunches of curls in her hair and a black and white dress. 'Thank you for this dress, I have never worn anything so pretty as this…'

'Any time… You look beautiful, Breland.' I knelt down and hugged her too.

'Oh, George. You ready? It's nearly time.' I stood back up and nodded as Grandad asked me the question which made me nervous even more.

'I'm ready.' Grandad put a white rose on my lapel, very similar to his. Everyone had left by then, so it was just me and him. 'Let's do this.'

***

'The Goth is here,' Security said into a radio device that sent a signal to the security to the castle. 'I repeat the Goth is here.' Just being said as we pulled up in the horse and carriage. One white horse wearing a black feather plumage, and one black horse wearing a white feather plumage on their heads.

'Grandad… I'm scared…' I said with a shaking breath. 'What if he walks off?'

'George, you are sixteen. You will have nerves like that. Look at me.' I picked my head up and looked at my grandfather. 'That wonderful man is going to love you his whole life. He has those nerves too! I did when I married Helen. It is natural, George.' I looked in front of me. 'Also, you are clean and sober today. This day will be amazing for you. Even if it's just for today you are clean and sober, this day will be amazing. Also, I made your cake. I don't want to eat it myself.' The horse and carriage came to complete stop. The lovely Leeds Castle was right in my view. 'This will be an amazing day.'

'Snow…' I looked out of the window fascinated by the snowflakes that were settling on all the surfaces they could find.

'Have you never seen snow?' I shook my head. 'Wow.'

'It's beautiful…' I noticed my grandfather has just got out of the carriage before me and held out his hand to help me out. 'Thank you.'

'Does that reassure you that he will not leave?' The tall, smart man pointed to an area with a birdbath, two priests, black and white flowers and two men in white suits with black roses on their lapels. One of them being Steyvan. 'Now. Let's get you married, young man.'

***

'George, your eyes…' Steyvan said in shock as I got to the altar. 'No drugs?' I nodded as he grabbed my hands. 'I am so proud of you, Mr Moth.'

'Save the kisses for later, you two. And save the flirting for tonight,' Kaz said, clad in cassock and collar having a laugh.

'Okay, Dad!' Steyvan said, laughing. I looked at the castle, the moat, then dead bolt into Steyvan's eyes. 'I love you, George…'

***

'Let's go back to my room…' Steyvan said with a grin and seduction in his voice after a small walk around the castle grounds.

'Actually… Can we take a small walk? I want to talk to you.' Steyvan nodded as I lead him into the front room of the castle which was closed off for the day for us. I brought him in for a hug and a kiss. I looked at my watch, then outside at the extensive area of greenery that the reception was being set up on ready for tonight. 'Steyvan, it's 3 pm. I have not had drugs or alcohol for twenty-four hours… I just—' I felt my voice going and a tear run down my cheek. 'I don't remember much due to the drugs and alcohol… But, I wanted to remember this day… Even if it's just today…'

'Babe!' He brought me in for a hug as I tried to settle my breathing, so I did not burst into tears. 'I am so, so proud of you!' He stroked my hair and kissed the top of my head. 'But, why twenty-four hours though? You could fuck yourself up, sweetie.' Steyvan picked up my head and brought me in for another kiss. 'But I am so, so proud of you…'

'It's so I remember… I don't remember much, but I wanted to remember this.' I held him close to me and put my head on his shoulder. 'Your vows were beautiful, by the way.'

'I loved yours too.' He slipped a piece of paper into my jacket pocket and I did the same. 'Let's go and get changed.'

'Changed? Not loved up?' I said, laughing through happy tears of marrying my one true love finally. He held me at arm's length. 'Well, that is putting it politely.'

'I didn't say we wouldn't, did I?'

***

I woke up from a small nap, snuggled up too my husband, remembering he put his vows in my suit jacket's pocket. I got up and grabbed the paper then opened it to see his vows:

My dearest George.

I remember meeting you for the first time. If anyone told me that I would be married to you in front of Leeds Castle, I would have told them that they were damn crazy. But, I am now marrying my best friend. I am so proud of how far you have come. From drugs galore to the young man I know today. From playing pub gigs to selling out at the O2 arena. Thank you for saying yes… What life would be without you, I don't know. I don't want to know. I just want you to know that for better or for worse, I will always be there for you. I love you, never forget that. I will always be proud to be your husband.

I smiled to myself, knowing that I am married to the love of my life. 'Steyvan… Wakey, wakey!'

'Huh… what?' He opened his eyes and smiled. 'Afternoon, Mr Vaughn-ray.'

'I love it when you say that,' I replied, smiling. 'Reception's in about an hour… It's 5 pm now.' I got on the bed and sat on his hips and rubbed his bare chest. Taking in the moment that he is officially mine.

'Can't wait! How you feeling now with no drugs and that, Mr Vaughn-Ray?' Steyvan said with seduction in his voice again.

'I feel fine… especially with you!' I got off his hips and smiled. 'I need to redo my makeup.'

***

'And let's welcome the newly-weds, George and Steyvan Vaughn-Ray!' I heard my grandfather say over a microphone. Steyvan and I walked into the marquee tent, which was filled with black and white decorations, guests, my mother and brother, Dodi, doing photography, my grandfather doing the food and then my grandma, Helen, along with Odette and Siobhan (and their bands) on the music. The current song was an old one but a good one. *Wake Me Up* by Wham! I grabbed Steyvan's hand and put my head on his shoulder as Dodi and my mother took photos of us.

'You look amazing, Steyvan.' I kissed him as Mum and Dodi got photos. 'Send that to me,' I asked them, well, rather requested them while giggling. Steyvan brought me in for another kiss as Grandad brought out a cake and I gave Steyvan a silly grin.

'Cake time!' Steyvan said, smiling ear to ear. 'You have the same idea as me, don't you?'

'I might! Let's just find out!' We cut the cake as Steyvan stood behind me with his right hand on mine (also my ring hand, as in Germany, we put the ring on the right hand) and his arm around my waist.

Photos taken, it was time to taste it. Strawberry jam with Victorian sponge.

'Go on then! Taste it!' I heard my grandfather yell.

'Ready!' Steyvan and I grabbed a piece of the black and white direct middle split cake. We held each other's cake pieces and laughed.

'You do! You have the same idea as me!' Steyvan said, laughing as we smashed the cake into each other's faces.

'If anyone has a video or pics of that, again, send them to me,' I said, trying not to cry of laughter while having my face covered in white icing and cake and Steyvan's face covered in black icing and cake. 'That is some lovely cake though.' I wiped my eyes clear, then Steyvan's before we both burst into laughter. 'Babe, you, uh… have a little bit of cake on your face.'

***

After we cleaned up, we went for the first dance. There was one song we both agreed on. *Colour by Numbers* by Culture Club. My grandfather actually managed to get Culture Club to perform! We held each other close and just stared at each other the whole time. It was just like we were the only two people in the world while the soundtrack to our life played in the background. Just a sweet, slow dance, allowing us time together in our own little world.

'I love you…' Steyvan whispered as I put my head on his shoulder.

'I love you too…'

***

Later that evening, after everything had wound down, we sat there just smiling away, slightly drunk. 'Let's go back, cuddle and sleep I think,' Steyvan suggested.

'I have a better idea!'

***

Chapter 11

'Happy anniversary, my love…' Steyvan said, waking me up by kissing my neck and pulling my ear lobe with his teeth.

'Happy anniversary, Steyvan… Not yet though… Wait till everyone is asleep tonight…' I said, letting out a small whimper.

'*Ja*, my love…'

'In fact… Now… Just be quiet.' He nibbled at my neck as I stifled my small whimpers of not relaxation, yet surprise.

***

'Well, Steyvan! That was a surprise!' I placed my head on his bare-naked chest and my hand next to my head.

'A nice dinner later! Then the staff meeting… Don't leave me, will you?' Steyvan asked me with a concerned tone.

'Why would I? Anyways. Let's get up, work a little and then go to dinner.' Steyvan nodded as I smiled and rubbed his bare chest. I sat up and looked at the door to see a female member of staff stood there. 'You okay?'

'Boss, someone wants to see you. Bethan, I think it is,' the tall, blonde, busty female said with a smile.

'Okay, let her into my office and tell her I will be there in five minutes. Ten tops.'

'Will do, sir,' she said, walking away, closing the door after her.

'Thank you, Cookie.' I grabbed my robe and put it around me to get up and get dressed quickly without anyone seeing me going commando for the day if staff walked in. I grabbed a black band t-shirt from one of my old tours and skinny black jeans. I quickly put my Stage Varsity jacket on with the band's logo on and got my ID card on around my neck.

'Makeup?' Steyvan asked, still lying in bed.

'Does it look like I am really bothered? I'm not today, babe. Get up. See you in a moment.'

***

I opened up my office to see Bethan sat there, looking scared out of her wits and shaking like a Chihuahua. 'Bethan, are you okay?' I asked her genuinely concerned. 'What's wrong?'

'I don't know… There is just so much pain…' I looked at her. 'It's just so bad and I'm so lonely too…' she said, wiping away tears.

'Women problems?' She nodded and sighed. 'The nurse can help there, but I could possibly help with the loneliness. Just someone there to chat to?'

'I would love that… Thank you…' she said under sniffles.

'I am available now till 12. I will be doing a little bit of work, but you are free to still chat to me.'

'Thank you…' she said, smiling shyly. 'So, how are you?'

***

'Well, Bethan, I best get going. Got to go to dinner!' I said, doing up my tie, and smiled, looking in the mirror at my all black suit. 'What do you think?'

'Looking very nice! Steyvan is one lucky man!' Bethan said, smiling. 'What is the occasion?'

'First anniversary!' I said, looking in the mirror, touching up my makeup.

'How old are you?'

'I'm 17 now,' I smiled, looking at the door seeing a shadow of my loving husband standing behind the door. 'Him? Well, he's 21.' I saw the door open after a lot of muffled swearing. 'Hello!' I turned around to see Steyvan in the doorway, in a white suit holding a black rose.

'Hello, George. Are you ready, my Gothic prince?'

'I am,' I said as he handed me the rose. 'It is lovely! Thank you…' He opened the door and let me through first. 'Bethan, I will come in and talk to you later. I will be back!'

***

'So, Steyvan. What is the plan for tonight?' I asked Steyvan in between eating bites of my dinner.

'Meeting when we get back and then a shag and sleep. NO DRUGS.' I smiled at him and chuckled slightly, 'What?'

'You! Being a debbie downer by saying no drugs!' I laughed putting my hand near Steyvan's.

'Hello, I am your drinks waiter. How may I help you, gentlemen? We can do beer, wine, champagne? What is suitable for your meeting? May I ask what you do?' A tall man asked us.

'We're here for our first wedding anniversary and me and my husband would love more of this wine please,' Steyvan asked with professionalism. The waiter laughed. 'Is there something wrong with us being gay?'

'That is so wrong!' I looked at the waiter with anger.

'I am going to the toilet. Before I do something, I shouldn't. I will be back, Steyvan.' I got up as the waiter still laughed. I clenched my fist as Steyvan looked at me. The waiter carried on laughing which riled me up so much to the point of punching his face. 'Is there anything wrong with us being gay? If so, let me kindly punch you in the face.'

'I am so sorry, sir!' our waitress said in her English accent while running over. 'Bradley! This is bad. You should NOT laugh at this!'

'It is fine.' I sat back down as Steyvan grabbed my hand to make sure I was okay and I nodded.

'It is on the house. More wine? So sorry.'

'That would be lovely. Thank you,' Steyvan said as the two waiters went away. 'You okay, George?'

'I'm fine.' The waitress came back over with three bottles of red wine and a smile. 'Thank you!'

'Take them. It's as a sorry. I'm lesbian. But not told anyone. Congratulations! One year being together for me and my girlfriend. Anyways. Enjoy your meal and wine,' she said to Steyvan and I with a smile.

'Congratulations! And thank you so much!' Steyvan said, smiling. 'And we sure will.'

'Thank you,' the waitress smiled and walked away.

'Oh. We have new clients!' said Steyvan, smiling.

'I will have to meet them,' I said, smiling. 'Let's finish, and get back. Then we can have the meeting and have fun…'

***

'OI! GUNNER! STOP CUTTING GARLIC TO PUT ON FUCKING PIZZA AND GET YOUR ASS IN HERE!' Steyvan yelled to the staff room. An olive-toned man with short black hair ran through. 'Alright. Staff meeting, we have more clients. Make them feel at home, correct medication needs to be dispatched morning, lunch and night. Any questions.'

'What if we can't?'

'Tough shit. You have to. Medication and making the clientele happy is our top priority. I'm very lax about the paperwork.'

'But, you can't expect us to drop everything,' the female said again.

'Trish, if you're just gonna be a fucking cow, you might as well fuck off,' Steyvan said as I sat there bouncing a ball against the wall. 'George, stop that.'

'Sorry, babe,' I said, smiling.

'It's okay. Just for now. Any other complaints? No? Okay. Get the fuck out. Carry on, George.' Everyone exited the room as I bounced my ball back onto the wall. 'Gosh… Staff!'

'Sweetheart. Calm down, okay? It will not do you any good.'

'I am calm now. Where's that bedtime fun you promised me?'

67

Dear Diary

Best anniversary ever. Infact. My first ever one celebrated. Now, to snuggle up to Steyvan!

G'night

George xxx

Chapter 12

I woke up at 6 am, like I normally do, got up and dressed and makeup done with breakfast. The usual. I got outside at about seven and went to my car. Finally passed my driver's test. *I'm happy! My Lambo is mine and legally...* For once... I mean I've been driving since I was twe' I will stop there. I opened the door and turned on the engine. I pressed a button to turn on the stereo and as it came on, heavy metal blared out. 'GOD'S SAKE.' I turned off the car and touched my pocket. 'I'll walk.' I took my iPod out of my pocket and put in my earphones. 'Hmmm. What to put on?' I went through my music and spotted all the classical composers. 'This will do me!'

***

I got to Morrison's as I saw one person I usually meet up with. Christine. A short, hyper woman. 'Morning, Christine!'

'I like Lorraine's partner's car. He's got a blue car.' I facepalmed and laughed.

'You still on that car?' She nodded, laughing cheekily. 'When are the rest getting here?'

'In about ten minutes! It's ten to eight!' I laughed and sat down opposite her on the floor in my big platform boots, makeup-less and hair up. 'Hey. How do you perform that in them?! They look heavy.' I jumped up as I saw another small woman come up.

'Quite easy, Christine. Normal shoes!' I took them off and put them in Christine's hands who laughed. 'Morning, Annette!'

'Morning, George! Long time, no see! Just waiting for Eileen. Can I leave my bags here?' Annette asked, standing there in her white body warmer, fluffy red top and black bottoms with simple trainers.

'Sure! I'll meet you in there!' Annette smiled quickly, put her bags down and shuffled into Morrison's. 'Is Eileen running late again?'

'Possible. Oh. I brought the milk.' I laughed and smiled. 'What?'

'You have not changed,' I said, putting my boots back on. 'The milk trick.'

'I don't like that milk from the little pots, I don't,' Christine said back to me. 'Let's go in.'

'Yeah, I need to pop to the little Goths room,' I said, grabbing Annette's bags and my bag. 'I'll put these with you.'

'Okay!' We got to the bench inside Morrison's and I put my bags down. 'Go on then, Goth. Go to the Goth's room!'

'I will! Gosh, Christine! Wanna smell my shoe?' Christine laughed very cheekily again, smiled again and pointing to the men's room. 'I'm going! Stop trying to get rid of me quickly, Christine!' I laughed, walking into the men's room.

***

'Talk of the devil and she shall arrive,' I said to Christine and Annette as a tall, grey-haired woman walked to us. 'Hello, Eileen!'

***

'I will see you all later!'

'Don't burn, George! You and your Vampire ways!' I flashed my fangs at Annette, Christine and Eileen and laughed. 'They are still awesome!' Annette said quietly.

'I won't burn! I don't burn unlike the sparkly freaks! I don't sparkle either. If you want proof, I'll get undressed.'

'No, save that for your husband!' Eileen said in her Lincolnshire accent.

'Bye, girls!' I said, walking away with my bags as everyone said goodbye.

***

'You okay, babe?' I heard as Steyvan came up behind me and hugged me. 'George?'

'I'm fine. Tired,' I said, yawning.

'Go to bed, George. Sleep.' I nodded as I trudged upstairs and sat on the bed. Next thing I knew, I slept till the gig.

***

Dear Diary

The gig went wrong, but I must've needed that nap!

Going to get drunk and high. In fact… No. I won't get high. BUT! I have been trying to show the real me. Steyvan said not to. But Eileen etc., don't mind.

Okay. Plan for the night—get drunk, bite Steyvan's neck (that's some nice blood), okay, I'm not actually a vampire. I just got the fangs from my dentist, and then get laid and sleep.

Gute Nacht.

George

***

Chapter 13

'Good morning, sweetie!' Steyvan said, walking into the office. 'You okay, George?'

'I'm fine. Just bored.' I grabbed a small bouncy ball and started bouncing against the wall and catching it. I saw in the corner of my eye, Siobhan walk in. 'Hey, Sib.'

'Get ready, George.' Siobhan said to me, smiling. 'We are going to dinner to meet someone.'

'Who?'

'Don't argue with me, George. Just get ready.' Grandma walked through as she wore a long flowy dress that complimented her fuller figure.

'Okay... Barkers is it?' I asked, intrigued. Siobhan nodded as Steyvan smiled. 'Okay. I'll be back.' I got up and walked out of the room.

***

'Let's go!' I said, smiling, all gothed up in platform boots, yet smart clothing, in a burgundy dress shirt and black suit bottoms and black makeup with my own brand, Skin Cling. The lipstick being liquid to matte, so it would NOT come off. I opened the door and walked out. 'You ready?' Everyone nodded and walked out with me of the sliding glass doors of the company. 'I'll be back, everyone!'

***

'So, who is this person?' I asked Grandma, Siobhan and Steyvan.

'Go in and you will see.' I walked into Barker's with my head down. 'Quicker! She ain't getting younger!'

'She?' Siobhan shrugged her shoulders. *It can't be Hara… She moved to Canada.*

'Hey, George!' A familiar voice squealed. I looked up and saw Hara standing there in a lovely blue kimono like dress that complimented her slightly fuller figure and her caramel curls. 'I've missed you!'

'I missed you too!' I said, trying to hold back happy tears. 'Still looking the same!' I dabbed my eyes quickly and sniffled.

'You DEFINITELY have not changed, George. Still the Goth I know and love.' I smiled and sat down. 'God! So much catching up to do!' Steyvan came in holding Darline in his arms and Siobhan holding Johnny's hand who was toddling along at his own pace. 'Are these your kids?! Oh they are too precious!'

'Thanks. The blondie is my husband. Steyvan. And I know you have met Siobhan and Grandma,' I said, sitting down opposite Hara. Her long, caramel-coloured hair just fell below her shoulders in bunches and bunches of curls. 'How is everyone?'

'Fine. Just, tired I think.'

'Hello, May I take your order?'

***

The drinks and food came and were eaten quickly and easily. Me and Hara caught up and made plans. 'Come on then! We have a spare staff slot for a councillor,' I said to Hara, smiling.

'Okay then, you've pulled my leg. Go on,' she smiled. 'Also, George, do you have any free slots available in your schedule? You know, the type that takes all afternoon in a hotel room?'

'I'm taken.' I laughed. I saw Grandma, Siobhan and Steyvan had gone back. 'Want to go to Costa?'

'Asda. The airport lost my case,' Hara sighed as her bright, brilliant blue eyes sparkled.

'Clothes are on me,' I said to Hara, smiling away. 'Just glad to have my best friend back.'

***

'So, do your kisses taste the same?' Hara asked me as we sat in Asda with a trolley full of clothes and shoes.

'Don't know. Want to try?' She kissed me and smiled. 'Do they?'

'Very. Still fruity!' She smiled at me like she did when I asked her out. 'So, how's your husband? I heard he was ill a few years ago.'

'He's over the cancer now, Thanks. Every now and then, he has what we call a "chemo" moment, so if you see him lying in a random place or sitting in a random place taking a nap, it will be that. We call them chemo moments because it's how he felt when he had the chemo.'

'I will keep an eye out. If it happens what should I do?'

'When he sits down, ask if he's okay, wants anything etc. and if he says no leave him for 20 mins from when he falls asleep and wake him,' I said, making sure she knew what to do. She nodded and smiled making notes on her phone.

'Okay. I will keep an eye out. He looked healthy.' I nodded in reply as I sipped a f'real strawberry milkshake. 'Bless him. What is he doing tonight?'

'Well, we have a gig and then, he will be out for the next two days.'

'Want to go back to old times? I just… really missed you.' Hara smiled and winked. 'I won't tell a soul.'

I thought about it for a few seconds. 'Deal.'

***

Gig over, Steyvan gone to his thing. Me, I was in bed with Hara… My ex-girlfriend… *FUCK. This will NOT end well will it?* 'Hey, Hara?' She lifted her head up and just looked glowing. 'What do you say, we just sleep and snuggle up?'

'Yeah, that's enough for me anyways, sweets. You're still good. Are you still taking drugs etc.?' I shook my head. Then nodded. 'We can work on that. How many lines a day?'

'One. I am getting there. Getting rid of it tomorrow.'

'Good. Night…' She clapped and the lights turned off.

'Night. Hang on. How do you know about that?!'

***

Dear Diary

LOVE TRIANGLE- Hara and Steyvan (my main boo). Who, just who to get with? Steyvan though… I will always be his and him mine. I'll stick with him.

Just can't believe Hara is back! Okay. I need to sleep, eyes are drooping.

Gute nacht

George
Xxx

***

Q&A!!!!!!

So, now you know some of my life, well. Half of it, let's do a little Q&A.

I asked a few people for questions. Here they are.

Q. Were you on any kind of drugs at the time?

A. Yes.

Q. What type?

A. Every single one.

Q. What made you turn onto drugs?

A. Foster parents.

Q. Were they awful and nasty to you?

A. I got thoroughly abused and I was forced drugs and alcohol.

Q. Did you ever get them done for the abuse they did to you?

A. Nope.

Q. Is that mainly because you were possibly scared of what they would do?

A. Oh yes. They could hurt me to shit.

Q. Do you feel it's them that have caused your depression and anxiety?

A. Oh yeah, but the anxiety? Not so much! I think the anxiety was caused by being caught more than anything.

Q. Do you kind of feel that why you want your kids to do so well in life and a great start due to what you went through yourself?

A. I don't want them having that. I don't want them having the life I had. It was horrid. I'm still recovering. I still want drugs. But, I won't touch them now. I and Steyvan have worked so hard to stop it, but I know, I will relapse. I don't want that for my kids.

Q. Where and when did you meet Steyvan?

A. I was at this black-tie formal event for musicians, and I saw him sat at the bar. I think I was about eight and he was about twelve, thirteen and he had a drink in his hand and he was just looking down and so I went over to say hi to him and he grabbed his bass bag and we chatted a bit, he gave me his number etc. and we hit it off from there.

Q. How many times can you get off in one night?

A. NO COMMENT. Everyone is different though.

Q. What's the record for your scream?

A. About 11 minutes so far.

Q. How many children do you have?

A. Two. Darline, who is the youngest and Johnny who is the eldest. And then, Steyvan's child Rose who is now 13 I believe.

Q. Would you adopt?

A. I would. Animal or child. I would.

Q. If you had all the money in the world what would you do with it?

A. Donate it to the charities that helped Steyvan during the cancer and also, pay off debts.

Q. Would you ever live in the jungle?

A. FUCK NO! Too many spiders and snakes. ERUGH!

Q. What are you scared of?

A. Nothing really. Just losing Steyvan. Oh. And spiders.

Q. What's your favourite thing to do?

A. COKE! Haha! Joke. I love to sit and play piano and just relax when I can. Whether it be playing Vivaldi or Bach or Beethoven or any classical composer, if you find me there, you know, I'm trying to get rid of all my troubles from that day.

Q. How did you get into the music you were in?

A. I grew up around Metal, but the classical side is awkward. I was looking through the CD store in Germany at the metal etc. and buying CDs and a piano song came on and I fell in love. I had quite a bit of money so I asked who it was, and the person said Bach. So I thought "okay." So I bought a CD and listened and I fell in love. Naturally, I wanted to learn the piano, so next gig pay I got, I bought a piano and self-taught myself Bach, Beethoven, Vivaldi, Mozart etc. Screamo/Metal however. Okay, ready? I was listening to metal, and my little foster brother, he bet I couldn't learn the song and do Screamo. So at school, I went into the rehearsal rooms, at home I went into the garden and learnt that Screamo song. Since then, I've self-taught my ways of not damaging my vocals and that lot and learnt from the likes of Amagortis, to Slipknot to Rammstein and I have even written my own songs for my own band The Deathbeds whom have been touring since I was 11 and my own classical music. Fun fact, I have been a child prodigy with piano AND Metal music and I have been put into a small "hall of fame" thing in Germany beside Rammstein.

Q: How did you come out?

A: I was basically caught being balls deep in a man's ass. Enough said I think.

I can't think of any more FAQ's, so here's a dear diary.

Dear Diary
  Go fuck yourself and your secrets.

George
Xxx

***

Chapter 14

'Boo. It's death coming to get you.'

***

Dear Diary

Worst nightmare EVER!

Steyvan died... God. I'd hate to think of that... It's a horrid thought. Life without him.

But hey! Working galore today!

Interviewing over 10 potential staff today!

Then paperwork. Got so much paperwork to do! Ugh... Murder me. TAKE ME, DEATH, NOT STEYVAN.... I'm the dumbass, he's not, haha!

Okay. Let's get on...

Fuck it. I'll write a little bit.

Now to do classical or Metal. CLASSICAL ALL THE WAY!

I love a bit of classical music. It relaxes me.

Okay.

Seriously going now.

SEE YOU LATER!!!

George

Xxx

Chapter 15

'I'm so sorry, Mr Vaughn-Ray… I am so sorry…'
   'No, no… Steyvan, wake up, please! WAKE UP!'
   'George… I am so sorry…'
   'FUCKING WAKE HIM UP!' I yelled with anger as they covered up Steyvan for dignity. 'WAKE HIM THE FUCK UP OR YOU WILL HAVE ANOTHER DEAD BODY TO DEAL WITH!'

***

'Whoa! You okay, George?' Steyvan said, putting his arm around me. I sat up crying my eyes out and started to put my black fluffy dressing gown on. 'George? Honey?'

'I'm not okay right now… I. You died…' I said to him, crying still but trying to talk so I make sense. 'You died, Steyvan…' I sat on the edge of the bed trying to calm down. 'It's time for me to get up anyways… I'll wake you up at eight…' I said, looking at the clock, 4 am. I am a bi-phasic sleeper aka I take a shit tone of naps.

'Okay, sweetheart… If you need me, wake me up earlier.'
'I will…'

***

'George? You okay?' I heard Hara say as she sat at the front desk. Her accent was just pure and sweet. 'I'm okay, Hara. Just a bit shaken up. I'm okay,' I smiled

'Well, had your insulin?' I replied with a simple nod. 'Well then, Oh. Bethan is in your office,' she said to me, pointing to the door of my office.

'Thanks, Hara. Another night tonight?' She smiled sweetly as I saw Steyvan come down the stairs shirtless and still in his pyjama bottoms.

'You okay now, George?' I nodded and smiled. 'Good. I'm going to go to the gym for a bit. After I get dressed, that is.'

'Okay, love.' I put my arms around Steyvan's neck as I kissed him. 'I'll be hanging about… Love you.'

'Love you too…' I put my head and hand on his bare chest and smiled as I stroked his skin. 'Don't leave me…'

'I won't I promise you, love… Now. I'll do press ups with you later… If you get me! Now, I will see you soon.' He stepped away from me smiling and walking away to go get dressed to work out.

'God… I'm… I'm going to talk to Bethan…'

***

'What's happening?' I asked myself as I lay on the bed stoned on lines and lines of cocaine and a little bit of meth. 'Fuck, I relapsed. FUCK!'

***

Dear Diary

This won't end well, will it?

I am stoned as hell. This could kill me. I already went into a coma once over drink and drugs…

Fuck, fuck, fuck, fuck, fuck, fuck. Okay. Sclera night… okay.

Just put them in. Okay. This should work. Oooh, my nerves are shot after that gig though that happened tonight.

He's just crawled into bed… Wish me luck! But, I will say, he's one hot mother! He's just very hot!

Okay, bed time for me!
Gute Nacht

George.

***

Chapter 16

Eighteen and LOVING IT! I've had a good gig, Steyvan is hot as hell and the company is bigger than ever! I'm with two record companies now! EEK! Let me take you through the day. Starting when I opened my eyes…

***

I woke up feeling happy as Larry (who the fuck is Larry?), looked next to me and saw a beautiful Steyvan lying next to me asleep. His blonde hair a mess, his beautiful bare, snow-white skin just glowing in the sunlight that peeped through the cracks of our black curtains. The black satin sheets just complimented his skin tone and how he slept… *God, I am one lucky man.* He was just lying there, asleep. *I best wake him up…* I thought to myself, smiling, taking one more glance to remember this heavenly moment. 'Steyvan…' I said to my loving husband, shaking him to wake him up. 'Morning.'

'Well! Good morning, birthday boy!' Steyvan said, sitting up slowly prior to giving me a major kiss. 'How is my darling today?'

'I am fine, big boy. How are you?' I straddled his hips and stroked his bare chest.

'I'm brilliant, George. Love you… What do you want to do?' Steyvan asked me as I winked. 'I like your style. But later… want a present?'

'Well. Yes… Is it a black ribbon this year?' I asked Steyvan as we burst out laughing after.

'No, no. But, it is black.' He gave me a set of car keys and smiled. 'This is just one, love. Many more later… And the pink ribbon is one of them!'

'I want black!' I laughed as Steyvan and I got the innuendo.

'Go on!' I got off of Steyvan's hips and sat on the edge of the bed, not letting anything show as I got dressed in a pair of black skinny ripped jeans and a black T-shirt with the tour dates of my band from two years ago in 2010! That was a shitty tour, anyways! I got a pair of black flats on to match. 'Slow down!' Steyvan said with a cheeky smile. I looked at the car keys and saw he had hidden the logo. He finished getting dressed and pointed to the door. I darted out and downstairs and past rooms to go outside. Steyvan followed behind laughing at me as I was like a little boy on Christmas day finally getting that red bike. I personally wanted a black one. 'Press the key.'

'Okay…' I pressed the open button on the car key and looked up as a black Mercedes Benz E-Class car unlocked. It had a blood red ribbon on it and a Happy Birthday banner in the windscreen. 'OH MY GOTH GOD,' I said, clasping my hands over my mouth before screaming like a little baby wanting a bottle. 'You serious?' Steyvan nodded quickly. 'You absolutely serious?' He nodded again. 'OH MY GOTH GOD!' I yelled followed by screaming. I calmed down and breathed. 'IN. WE'RE GOING FOR A FUCKING RIDE!'

***

'Oh my God. That runs like a beauty!' I said to Steyvan, looking at the all black interior. 'Like the lambo, this is my baby.'

'I thought it would be!' Steyvan said, laughing as we got out of the car. 'Many more to come, love.'

'That's what she said,' I said, trying to stifle a laugh after but completely failing. 'Sorry,' I said, laughing my head off.

'Ah, you are too adorable,' Steyvan said, wrapping his arms around me and pulling me into a kiss. 'GO, GO, GO!' I heard Steyvan yell behind as I got shot at with nerf guns when he broke the hug.

'FUCKING HELL!' I said, protecting myself with my hands. 'IT'S ON LIKE DONKEY BLOODY KONG, BITCHES!' I grabbed the nearest nerf gun I saw and put my sunglasses on. 'Bring it, bitch.'

***

'God that was epic!' I said to Steyvan as I sat down after the most epic nerf gunfight ever. '*OH! EISBRECHER!*'

'English.'

'It's a band... Oh well. So, what else is planned for today?' I asked Steyvan, wrapping my arm around his chest as I placed my head near his heart. 'I love hearing your heartbeat...'

'A nice dinner. Maybe a walk etc... Up to you, birthday boy!' he said, smiling away. 'And why? Why do you like listening to that?'

'No idea. I think it is a comfort thing,' I said, smiling away. 'Wanna nap?' Steyvan nodded. 'Just for like an hour... Then we'll have fun.'

***

'PEW! PEW!' I heard from my son as he shot me with nerf guns.

'OI! YOU LITTLE SHITEBAG!' I got up and grabbed my nerf gun. 'JOHNNY! COME HERE!' I shot him with my nerf gun as he ran away giggling away. 'HAHA! GOT YA! Now. Pick up the bullets.' I looked at Johnny and laughed.

'Happy birthday, Dad!'

'Thanks! It's Christmas soon!' I said to him, smiling. 'I'll take you out. I know I have been a shit dad lately. Sorry, mate.'

'Dad, it's okay. You have a lot going on. Don't worry,' Johnny said as he finished up picking up the nerf gun bullets. 'It's life.'

'You will go far, kid.' He rolled his eyes as he walked back to the lobby and into the staff room. 'You really will...'

***

Later that day, well, let's just say, I had a brilliant time. A lovely romantic dinner, a walk along the beach, a snuggle and a kiss… Brilliant day. I put my head on his shoulder as his fingers interlaced with mine. 'Thank you, Steyvan… It has been a lovely day.'

'Any time, love. You deserved it.' We walked along the pier as the sun started to set. 'Don't let me go, Jack…'

'You freak. I love that about you…'

***

Later that evening, I sat there at the front desk sorting out things and paperwork quick. 'George, to the ballroom. That is George Vaughn-Ray to the ballroom. Steyvan needs your help with the set up.' I heard the tannoy say. 'Okay then…' I walked to the ballroom and I looked around. 'Steyvan? I'm here.'

'SURPRISE!' Everyone yelled, making me jump as I opened the door to the ballroom.

'HOLY SHIT!' I said, jumping out of my skin. 'Thank you all so much!'

'George! I need your help.' Steyvan said, walking to me.

'I'm coming!' I walked to the ballroom and opened them to a simultaneous "SURPRISE!" from everyone and eighteen banners and balloons everywhere. 'Thank you, guys!'

'You deserve it! Oh! Happy birthday!' Steyvan said, handing me a large box. 'Will you stop complaining now?'

'Why?' I opened the box which revealed platforms that I always wanted. Knee high, 8-inch platforms. 'OH MY GOD! HOW THE FUCK DID YOU AFFORD THESE?! LET ALONE KNOW!'

'You sent enough fucking emails with them linked to everyone on the bottom "George Vaughn-Ray P.S Hint Hint." followed by the bloody link, George.'

'Oh! I did,' I said, laughing. 'They are beautiful! Thank you so much!'

'Glad you like them.'

'Like?! Fucking LOVE them!' I said with exaggeration on the love. 'Oh, can't wait to get these on… For now, let's dance.'

***

After a dance and a hug and a few, other things, we decided it was time to go to bed. It was the best day of my life. Honestly… without this opportunity of a great day, I think I would've committed suicide on my 18th… Steyvan changed that.

***

Dear Diary

Today was the best birthday I think I have ever had. Steyvan made it all better, and to top it off, I got more platforms that I have ALWAYS wanted that were like what? £1,000?! They are beautiful! From the moment I woke up to now, it was a darling experience.

From the moment I woke up to now, I haven't wanted to kill myself. And I still don't… Seems being with Steyvan was a blessing in disguise.

I believe in love at first sight. And, that was it with Steyvan. When I first spotted him sat there at the bar, all alone with a drink in his hand and his bass next to him, I knew he was the one. He looked smart, was so polite and helpful… Even pointed the way to the little Goth's room!

Now look at us. We're married, own a company and more. I just, am really thankful for him…

Fuck, that is too soppy for me.

Here's something I would usually say: Fuck you.

Gute Nacht

George

***

Chapter 17

'Okay, Steyvan's twenty-three… Okay,' I said to myself as I sat there at the desk, relaxing.

'Morning, babe,' I heard him coming from the door.

'Morning, birthday man! How old are you today?' I asked for a laugh.

'EIGHTEEN AND A VIRGIN!' he yelled out before bursting into laughter. I shortly joined him. 'Actually, I'm sadly 23.' I looked at him as he giggled and sat at his desk. Ready and dressed for the day. 'I don't want to do anything today… Just had a chemo moment and it was not nice. How's the girls down at Morries?'

'Didn't go today. I'm going tomorrow.' Steyvan nodded. 'Yeah. I've spoken to Eileen though. She's Okay,' I sneezed and smiled.

'Bless you, honey! That was so cute! I may go back to bed in a moment… I am so tired after that moment.'

'If you need to, go ahead. You look knackered.'

'I am… I'll see you later, love.' He got up and came to kiss me. 'Love you.' He kissed me as it left a lingering feel on my lips.

'Love you too.'

***

Two hours later, Steyvan came back looking tired, but better as he sat down at his desk and started typing up some bits. 'So, how you feeling now?'

'Better…' he said, looking up from his typing. 'Can I have a hug?'

'Come here then,' I said, smiling as Steyvan rolled over on his chair over to me. 'Bless ya.' I hugged him as he put his head on my shoulder. 'You look adorable…' I put a box in front of him. 'Hope you like it, I know it's not much, but you know. I do have more though… But it's the thought that counts.' He opened the box to reveal a Swarovski crystal diamond ring and necklace cross set.

'This is lovely! Thank you, George!'

'Will you re-marry me? As sober, clean me.'

'YES!'

***

Dear Diary
Today went so well and smoothly. HE SAID YES!
Gute nacht <3

George

***

Chapter 18

So, I thought I would share some letters that Steyvan and I wrote to each other. We were not always lovey-dovey. But we were old-fashioned in the way of letters. We always wrote letters instead of anything else to each other. We found it very romantic. Okay, sometimes they were about our fights or just a small message to help each other through the day.

One of the best ones—in my opinion that is—about our fighting was one Steyvan wrote when we were in a bit of a mood. He sat there, pissed off to hell, and I was doing some work and he slipped a note onto my desk that said "Fuck you cunt. Talk to me, you fucking sheep fucking lion fucking shagging fucking mother-fucking-fucker." And I was just unphased, so I said hi to him and he just blanked me. That was why it made the best for that one, but I tell you what. I will put it into subjects and have a few on each subject! In no random order!

SUBJECT ONE!!! Gigging

Now, I know this is a random subject. But here is a random convo I and Steyvan had by letter. It makes me laugh because of his end letter that finished this off.

Me: Babe, we have a gig at H&H tonight!

Steyvan: Oh yeah? What is the set list?

Me: The usual, The Smoke, Heil Hitler. Blah de blah de blah. What we did last year on tour.

Steyvan: Ah okay! Lemme play your bass string? ;)

Me: No…

Steyvan: Your mouth?

Me: Innuendos r us!

Steyvan: OKAY! OKAY! How about a good shag behind the drum riser?

Yeah. That happened. Now you know why it ended quick.

SUBJECT 2!!! Love

Okay. I'll only just do these two subjects. Most of them are so personal. Here's one Steyvan sent after I was a hormonal wreck and upset to the point I nearly had a panic attack.

Dear George

You should never give up. I know it's before a gig. BUT, as I keep saying, once you start, you can't stop. But you can resist, and that resistance is key. The key to life... Just remember that, love. You are doing too well to give up. You are the best metal singer the world has. ABOVE slipknot. YOU have been awarded the heavy-metal hall of fame for fuck's sakes. Is Corey Taylor etc. in there?! FUCK NO! YOU ARE! You should never give up!

But someone once told me that love is hard to describe... It is not. Love to me is you and the way you show it. Everyone has different ways. Your way is quirky and kooky. You buy me makeup, jewellery etc. Not the usual, dinner etc. We are NOT like that. We just like a cute snuggle and a chat.

I love you, George. Never forget that. No matter what happens, you will always be the best.

You can do this.

Lots of half makeup kisses

Steyvan xxx

I ALWAYS keep this letter on me. It gives me courage and a smile. I love you, Steyvan. More than you will ever know.

***

Dear Diary.

I'm 19, legal, sexy and ready! I have so much on my plate though!

I HAVE A RECORD DEAL FOR CLASSICAL AND METAL!!! EEK!

Okay. Bed time.

Gute Nacht

George

***

Chapter 19
Garcia

I woke up to the Englishman, called Kaz, I called my partner, and went downstairs in my slippers and black fluffy dressing gown to see my dad, Tim, sat there with Mum as Dad was trying to calm down. 'Everything okay?' I asked Mum as she hugged Dad.

'I'll be back in a moment, Tim, okay?' My dad nodded as Mum took me aside. 'Garcia... I am so sorry... He's just lost his brother... Just give him time and space.' I nodded as I looked to Dad. 'What you up for?' I looked at the time. 'Can't sleep?'

'No... Kaz was snoring,' I said to Mum as Dad plonked his head down on the table.

'Game of Cards Against Humanity?'

***

'The school trip was ruined by Blank,' my dad read out from a black card as I looked through my white cards to choose. 'OOOOH!'

'Oh God,' Mum said as we both put a white card down at the same time.

'Oh, God is right!' I said to Mum, laughing my head off.

'Okay!' Dad said, picking up the white cards. 'The school trip was ruined by touching a pug on his penis. Okay then. The school trip was ruined by dead babies?! OH, DEAR GOD! THAT ONE WINS!' Dad yelled while trying to not laugh his head off. I raised my hand as I put my head on the table laughing. 'You sick cow.'

'That's me! Okay! Make a Haiku.' The parents took a while to look at the cards. Dad put his down first followed by Mum. 'Okay! Kanye West, Riding off into the sunset, some goddamn peace and quiet. That's EPIC! Boners of the elderly, sexual humiliation, depression. Ohhh, this is hard. I think the Kanye one.' Dad raised his hand nearly pissing himself laughing. 'That one is brilliant!' I sat there laughing, finishing off my glass of wine as Kaz came down. 'Another round?'

***

It was 7am and I just woke up on the sofa from an intense game of Cards Against Humanity. I saw Mum and Dad asleep on the other sofa beside us. Kaz had his arm around me as I slowly slipped out of bed to try not to wake him up. After a cup of coffee, waking Dad up for his medication and my medication and clearing up some bits, I got dressed and ready for college. 'You going to see George later?' Dad asked me as I nodded. 'Okay. Pop by to cookery and I will have a huge batch of brownies for you!'

'Oh! I love those brownies!'

'Get your arse moving. Want me to drop you off? 'Cause you need your bass and violin, don't you?'

'Fuck, I do,' I said, grabbing my bass bag and two violin cases.

'Get in the car. I'll take you!'

***

After the most pathetic day at college, I got to George's house. 'George?!' I let myself in with the spare key and put my stuff down in the hallway.

'UPSTAIRS!' I heard George yell down. 'I'LL BE DOWN IN A MOMENT! I'M A BIT NAKED!'

'Okay!' I looked around and saw Steyvan lying on the sofa flicking through BBC iPlayer. 'Hey. You okay?' Steyvan nodded.

'I'm cool. Just feel like utter crap.'

'Get used to it!' I laughed. 'Had a good day?'

'Slept most of it,' he said, putting the remote down and sitting up. I sat next to him as he tapped the sofa. 'Oh well. How was college? I heard it was shit.'

'Shit ain't the word! Got bollocked twice, nearly suspended, fell over three to four times, nearly broke my ankle,' I said as Steyvan winced. 'Yeah. But, on the bright side, I got brownies.'

'OH! What type?! Are they weed brownies?' I shook my head and laughed. 'Ah fuck. I tried.' He sat up and laughed more as George came through. 'Hey, babe.'

'Hey, Steyvan. Heya, Mama. What brings you here?'

'Is a mother not allowed to see her son anymore?' George smiled. 'I just came to see how you were. Try skank a dinner off you too. I can't be arsed to cook, also I just wanna catch up with you two.'

'That's cool,' Steyvan said.

'You okay?' George asked me, intrigued. I nodded. 'You just look in pain.'

'I am a little bit… I'm just wondering about your man! He looks like shit. You okay? You look… really weak.'

'I'm okay. Really. I am just knackered,' he smiled at me as I looked to George stroking a fluffy dog.

'What type of dog is that? Jesus! He's like a proper massive fluff ball. A cotton ball that grew a face!'

'Samoyed Husky mix,' I smiled as the dog lay down on George's lap.

'Bless! Want a card game of Cards Against Humanity?'

***

'I best get going. I will see you lot later! Hope you feel better soon, Steyvan.'

'I should do. Thank you so much. See you soon, Garcia.'

'Love you, mama!'

***

I got back home and snuggled down into bed due to my back as Kaz came in. Hair newly dyed and in rollers. 'Shit! Garcia! Why are you home?!"

'I… I was really in pain… Why? What? Are you?' I said as I looked at him in shock.

'I was going to tell you, Duck! I am so sorry… I just… didn't feel right as Kaz any longer… I am so, so sorry, Duck… Forgive me,' Kaz said to me as I sat on the bed in shock. 'I am so sorry…'

'As long as you don't nick my undies, I'm cool with it, Kaz… Why didn't you tell me sooner?'

'I thought you'd hate me.'

'Why would I?'

'Because I've not told ya, Duck.'

'I wouldn't hate you! Because… I am trans too.'

***

Dear Diary
> *Mum is right…Steyvan does look ill. Just hope he is okay.*
> *Gute Nacht*

George

***

Chapter 20
One Year Later

It was 2016. I did my usual routine without Steyvan. (When he's here, it's wake up, cuddle, kiss, get n—not going any further.) Get up, have a shower, shave, dry off, do hair and makeup. The normal. I got to work, but when I went inside, it was different. Staff were on point and present, all clients fed and medicated. A grown up 12-year-old in a suit came up and hugged me. 'Morning, Johnny. What's going on?'

'Morning. Why?' my son said to me smiling away.

'Nothing, I'm just wondering as staff are never usually this productive,' I said to Johnny. 'So, how about a good old-fashioned chat, son?'

'I need to get on, Dad, sorry.' I looked at him and smiled. 'Maybe later though! Where's pappy?'

'He is at the gig. He's um… He's okay… just very worn out, matey,' I smiled as he nodded. I walked to my office and opened the door with my staff ID card that I had on my belt. I walked in and dumped my bag next to me as I sunk into my chair. I noticed a few changes. Paperwork was tidied, pens and pencils were in the right place, the whole lot. Then my eye caught a little, bright neon pink square note saying "FOUR" in Steyvan's handwriting. 'What the—? Oh well.'

'George?' I heard a timid small voice coming from the other side of the door. 'I need to talk to you…'

'Come in!' I said, looking at my emails. 'Everything okay?' I said, looking at the female staff's face. She looked down and upset.

'Um… I've been told to give you this and to tell you to get to the hospital…'

'What?' She shrugged as she ended me an envelope with my name on it. 'What the… Emaly. Tell me what's happening?'

'I don't know, George. That's all I have been told.' I nodded as I opened the envelope.

'To my Gothic love, Georgie.

I have to come clean. I wasn't too honest with you. When I was 16, they gave me the all clear… But, it came back two years ago, they've just declared it terminal… I am so, so sorry. I just did not want to upset you, my Goth moth king. I am still in shock really. Treatment? I've stopped it. I've stopped chemo and radio. They give me one more year at the latest. I should see you turn 22… I am so very sorry, sweetie… Just remember this. I LOVE YOU. I will collect you… You have been my soulmate all my life. You have been there for me all the time I was ill. I'm just sorry I didn't come clean, sweetheart. Don't be too upset. I'll look after Jansn and Thomhas for you… Move on when I do. You are strong. You are NOT weak. Just keep clean for me. Also. FOUR.

Lots of half-faced makeup love and kisses

Your king, Love

Steyvan
Xxx'

'Oh God no. Oh dear God no!'

'George? What's wrong?' I let out a very quiet scream as I realised why I needed to go up to the hospital… My worst fear has come true. 'George? Come here…' Emaly walked over to me and hugged me. 'What's up?'

'STEYVAN IS DYING!' I said, screaming, letting my cries get louder.

'Oh, sweetheart… Want someone to come with you?' I shook my head until Hara came in dressed and ready to take me. 'Hara's dibbed apparently.'

'Hey, honey…. Come on. It's all going to be okay… I'm here.'

'Let's go… He can't die…'

***

'Steyvan… Don't leave me, honey.'

'I am so sorry I didn't tell you, George… I didn't want you to know…'

'It's fine…' I said, wiping tears away from my cheek.

'Take my ring off and put it on your finger…' I did what he said as he then put a little statue in my hand. "From our wedding…' I scooped him up in my arms for a kiss. We kissed as he smiled weakly after. 'I… Love… You…' I felt him go limp.

'No, no. Steyvan, Wake up. DO NOT DO THIS TO ME!' A Nurse put her hand on my shoulder as reality hit me. 'What was it? Just tell me…' I said underneath the waterfall of tears with my head buried into my only love's cold chest.

'Testicular… George… I am so sorry… How about, you go home, try to calm down and we will get him sorted into a chapel of rest. You can sleep in there, the lot, until it's time…' I shook my head. 'Okay… The offer is always there.'

'I wouldn't have been able to do it. It's all too much for me with that…' I said, lifting my head up. I let go of his hand as Hara hugged me.

'George, honey, I don't know what to say that will make you feel better. BUT I know what I CAN do to try at least make it a bit better. Black ice cream.'

'That exists?' the nurse said with a chuckle as I kissed Steyvan's hand. I closed my eyes and said a little prayer for both of us. I am not religious in a way, but he was. I believe in good and evil and prayer, and that is as close as to religion I get, which, Steyvan did accept.

'I love you…' I let go of his hand and walked out of the room holding back a lot more tears.

***

'George? Honey…' I heard Hara's voice say from behind me as I looked out from the smoking area of the hospital. 'George…'

'Fucking leave me alone, Hara. I want to be alone,' I said, looking at the little trinket with my cigarette in my other hand. 'Just… Please. Leave me be…'

'Okay… Just be careful, okay, George?' I nodded as I carried on looking at the little trinket. 'Okay… I'll come back later.'

'Okay, Hara…' I stared at the little object in my hand that symbolises Steyvan's and my first kiss as a married couple. 'God, why didn't you take me instead of him… I had cancer too. He's too fucking sweet to leave this earth…'

'Because the best ones go first sadly,' I heard Steyvan's voice say.

'WHAT THE ABSOLUTE FUCK?!' I yelled as I jumped. 'Where the fuck did that come from?'

'I said if I die, I'll be here. So I am by your side. And I also said that I will be here for you. I will never leave your side as I promised to haunt your ass, sorry, love you forever… did I not?'

***

Dear Diary

Today? Today was fucking horrible… I've lost part of me, part of the band, my son's father, my daughter's father, half of my heart… Can't believe Steyvan died… I really can't… Just wish he told me. Oh well, what's done is done. I am going to try and relax… Might knick his top he wore for bed… Hug his pillow and blanket… See what comforts me the most.

Gute Nacht

George…

***

Chapter 21

Seven years passed, I grew more and more depressed... became an alcoholic and relapsed on drugs until Hara stepped in.

'George?' I picked my head up as she crawled into bed next to me. 'You need to move on, honey... Or cheer up at least.'

'Hara, I have had two hip replacements, I'm 27 and I have two artificial hips. I have lost the pure love of my life seven fucking years ago. They reckon it takes four to EIGHT years to get over trauma like that. Don't fucking tell me to cheer up or move on.' I turned around so my back was facing her. 'Night,' I said bluntly. I waited till she fell asleep to get up. I slowly sat up, making sure I didn't wake her and I finally got out successfully. I walked to my office and put my head on my table. I saw paper, grabbed a piece and began to write with a pen I found on my desk.

To Johnny

You now own the company.

By the time you have read this, I will be with your father, Steyvan.

You are a good, mature, young man.

All details, cards and everything you need to know are on my computer, my desk and in the files.

I love you.

'Goodbye…' I grabbed all my medication and took them all in one go. 'Goodbye…' I closed my eyes and went to sleep as I drew my final breaths.

***

Dear Diary

GOODBYE.

***

Epilogue
Johnny POV

'Dad?' I said, knocking on the door before opening it. 'Dad?' I repeated, thinking he was in the toilet. I saw him asleep in his chair in a white suit. *I'll leave him to sleep for a while.* I walked out and kissed my girlfriend, Eleanora. 'Hello, sweetums! Want to go out?' I looked at her and pushed her beautiful blonde hair out of the way. I looked into her deep beautiful brown puppy eyes as she nodded. 'Where to? A good ol' fashioned Costa?'

'Oh. yes! I would love that!'

'Let's go!' I grabbed my car keys and smiled at her, knowing Dad was safe just really tired. 'Glad Dad is sleeping... He certainly needs it.'

'Bless. He's been on his feet. Worried about the anniversary. Anyways, let's go out and enjoy.'

***

We finally came back at 3pm after a Costa Coffee in the heart of town. I kissed Eleanora once more getting out of the car. 'Go check on your dad, Johnny. Wake him up,' Eleanora said to me in her sweet posh English accent.

'You read my mind! I'll meet you here.' I kissed her and walked to Dad's office, knocking before entering. He'd lost colour and there was a note for me on his desk and an empty bottle of pills. 'Oh shit,' I put my hand over my mouth in shock. 'One, before I freak out that you're dead and do all the precautions, white is NOT your colour. Okay. Okay. Calm down, Jonathan.' I looked at Dad, he looked like he was in a deep peaceful sleep. I looked on his desk and looked at the date of the pills. 'Okay they are yours, but issued today… Oh God… Not this day. Not the anniversary.' I grabbed the note and walked out of the room. I walked up to Eleanora and hugged her.

'What's wrong, Johnny? You okay?' I shook my head and broke down in tears. 'What's wrong? Johnny? Talk to me.'

'The Goth is down…' I struggled to say through the waterfall of tears. 'Dad's gone…' I wiped my tears away and breathed as I opened the letter.

To Johnny.

You now own the company.

By the time you have read this, I will be with your father, Steyvan.

You are a good, mature, young man.

All details, cards and everything you need to know are on my computer, my desk and in the files.

I love you.

'Dear God no.'

'Johnny, I am so sorry, sweetheart,' Eleanora said as her arms went around me to comfort me. 'Sweetheart. Just think this, yeah? If you do anything stupid, who is he gonna annoy and piss about with?'

'Dad… in heaven 'cause I'm going to fucking hell!' I said in mid-stream of tears.

'Why do you say that? Oh, sweetheart.'

'I didn't keep an eye on him,' I said, throwing my arms around her.

'Johnny… don't put yourself down. How were you to know this was happening? Come here, sweetheart.'

***

Years later, the company was thriving. I was in my late 20s. Doing my dad proud! 'Johnny?' I heard from the door.

'Yes, sweetheart?' I said, turning around to see my beautiful wife, Eleanora. 'You okay?'

'I'm pregnant.'

***

An Unseen Dear Diary

My father always shared his Dear Diaries… apart from a few and I was flicking through it. It was a tradition of his to write one every day and night. Most of them didn't catch my eye until I came across a long one, full of letters to him. I thought I'd share it. It shows how much love he has for his family and that, and his clients too. I miss him a lot. But, my grandmother could bring him back. I don't want to put her through her old Wiccan ways. What's done is done… Well, here is that "Dear Diary" I promised. Enjoy.

'Dear Diary,

Well, you have me in a loving mood!

God, his hair, his eyes, his body, his face, everywhere else, if you get what I mean! I love it all! He's beautiful, yet psychotic.

But not in a bad way. Oh no. In a very good way. He'll say "I love you" to me or act all offended then kiss me and just kiss my neck and tease me by pulling away and going to his desk opposite mine. Or, he'll sit on the bed next to me, say something and his eyes will have mischievousness in them and he'll just pin me to the bed and I will go no further ;) but it's a good psychotic. Never a bad way with him… Unless you really piss him off. Then he'll go all badass on you. But, he's just perfect in every way, well,. in my terms! Not everyone says he's good for me. But, I know he is. He's a perfect little sweetheart, my son's father too… That perfect English accent, the 6 packs and it's not of beer. He proposed when I was 14. Then our daughter, helped by Jeremy, my bands guitarist, came along and helped. I'm now 19. Legal in most countries to have sex… WHY GEORGE. YOU HORNY BASTARD!!!! GOD, DUDE! Anyways, I can now travel without adults, is that a wise idea? I'm clean of drugs for the most part and I own Vaughn-Ray LTD with Steyvan. He just walked into the room shirtless. COME TO PAPA! Sorry, it's just a really hot sight. And he's gone. He just wanted a new top. Well, if he just got out of the shower, I would've needed new jeans ;) Okay. I WILL STOP.

Anyways. In other news, got letters from the family today. Here are just some of my thoughts.

From Odette;

"HEY BRO!

How's it going? OMG I HEARD YOU OWNED IT TOO! CONGRATS BRO!!!! I'm not pregnant. Just fat. But the Boy George career is going well for me! Has been for years. We really need to meet up! I'm in Grantham touring with Culture Chameleon soon, so wanna meet up? If so, gimme a bell and I will be there ASAP!
Give my love to everyone!

Lots of love
Odette, AKA Boy Reid
xxxxxxxxxxxxxxxxxxxxxxxxxxxxxxxxxxxxx"

My opinion on Odette? Too hyper! But, I'll meet up with her.

From Dodi though;

"Dear Anolin
Broke my hand again

From Dodi."

DODI YOU ACCIDENT-PRONE PRICK! I'M JUST GONNA FUCKING WRAP YOU IN BUBBLE WRAP! YOU TWAT!

From Dad, he's dyslexic so I will do it how he wrote it then translate;

"Two George.

Ive bin to Melton twoday wif your Mover. Newark twomorrow. Knot much two sai reallie. Fineally seaing her speshalist soon, will keep u updayted.

Oh! Eileen will bee 'ere wif me four thee weak! U will meat her!

Sea u soon.

Kazarian. Xxx"

Basically, when he wrote it, he went to Melton for the day, going to Newark the day after, not much to say but finally seeing the specialist and he will keep me updated. Bless him. He is trying at least. About two months ago, he wouldn't even ATTEMPT to write a letter.

This one, it's from someone near and dear to my heart. My Mother, Garcia;

"Heya son

How are you doing? How's Steyvan? How's the kids? Here, don't believe what your father says. Everything is okay, been out, been about. Just feel like shit. But hey, its life!

Hope to hear back from you soon son! It's been too long!!!

Love you

From
Your Mother xxx"

I love you, Mum. More than you will ever know.

But I did get a few from clients and more. I won't do the clients. Apart from one. Bethan. She came in when she was 15. She's now 16. Here it is! From Bethan;

"Thank you George, thank you for all that you have done. I appreciate it so much! I know, we shouldn't write letters etc. to you. But, I didn't know how else to express my thanks for you teaching me English etc. Thank you so much."

Now, that one did really make me smile. Letters like that just really make me smile.

I'll leave the letters there or this whole diary will be just letters!

But another thing that's on my mind? The bullshit that's in this world. There's too much.

Anyways, I best get to bed. Get my happy as Larry ass to bed. (WHO THE FUCK IS LARRY?)

Gute Nacht!

George.'

See what I mean? It shows so much love, so much grateful emotions coming from him, just from a little letter. That's the thing I loved about my father... You even gave him the slightest "I love you" note or a hug, he was so grateful.

I will leave this here...
Good night.

Johnny
xxx

Love Endures

Prologue

'George… George Vaughn-Ray?' I said, for perhaps the first time, nervously to the person at the big iron set gates with ivory toning. 'Is this cotton candy?'

'No, sorry George. This is cloud. Do you know where you are?' An angelic-looking man wrapped up in a toga said to me laughing in his Scottish accent. I shook my head as I went to touch it. 'Don't eat it. Trust me. And you are in heaven.'

'Oh…' I replied pleasantly shocked. 'Can I ask something? Please?'

'Being as you politely asked, yes. Yes, you may, George.'

'Is Steyvan here?'

'He is, George. Very popular too! Time goes quick. Find him as quick as you can… Go on, George! I shall see you around,' the voice with Scottish accent rung out pointing to the gates which opened.

'Thank you… Any idea on location?' He shook his head. 'Thank you.' I walked through the gates, as they shut behind me. I turned my head and looked to see wings. 'What are these feathery things?' I saw they were black and white. 'That is the least of my worries.' I walked what looks like a street… of clouds. 'What in the heck is going on here? Hang on. Good. Can't say that h word. That's most of my vocabulary gone I guess.' I looked to my right. A park full of black roses, with white and red.

'Are you new?' I heard a voice come from behind me. I turned around to see a nice, smiling female in white with ivory wings. 'I'm Taylor. Most call me Tay.'

'George… George Vaughn-Ray,' I said shyly yet with relief.

'The George Vaughn-Ray? Like the George Vaughn-Ray to Steyvan Vaughn-Ray?' I nodded. 'He says so much about you at his gigs!'

'That's good... Um... Can you help me please? You are the first face I have seen since I got here... Do you know where he is, or the way to civilisation?'

'Can you fly?' I shook my head. 'Damn... I can't help you then... Sorry, George. But if I see him on my travels, I'll let him know you are here. If you need food, the trees are edible, as are the flowers! Just, don't eat the clouds. As funny as the side effects are, it's not pretty for the one suffering those side effects!' Taylor laughed as I looked at her worried. 'The side effects are, but not limited to the following; Excessive glitter farts, projectile rainbow vomiting, wanting to drink too much because of said rainbows, pooping out ice cream, and yes, that includes the cone, seeing stars and your head comes off and floating like cotton candy... though luckily that last one doesn't last long.'

'How do you know that?' I questioned Taylor.

'First-hand experience.' Taylor said embarrassed. 'It's funny until it happens to you.'

'So a bit like going outside when its icy, people skid etc, it's funny. Then you do it and it's not funny?' I said before laughing a little bit.

'Exactly like that. Also, what do you see here? They say that here shows flowers relating to their happiest memories. I see red tulips and white carnations, my favourite flowers.'

'Thank you. And, um... well, I see black and white roses... Steyvan and I had them at the wedding,' I said, intrigued.

'That's what Steyvan saw! With the pop of red.' I smiled. 'If you need help, just whistle. Like you would a dog. I know about you and your 27 pugs. But, just whistle. Someone will be with you. Oh, also, I do know you were diabetic. You do not have that here, if you want chocolate, eat it!'

'Thank you, Taylor.' she waved goodbye and walked off. 'Right...' I saw the tree Taylor was on about and looked at the apples. 'Oh that's nice! That will be good.' I looked around to see a mirror like surface on a wall. I was wearing a white suit, black tie and my good old platforms with no makeup. 'Oh my word... flawless skin. Bonus.'

***

A day had passed, Taylor came back in. 'Are you a flightless angel?' she smiled.

'Oh, Jesus,' I jumped. 'Yeah, it seems so, Taylor.' I smiled.

'Not the only one!' I ruffled my feathers on my wings, which sent some of my black feathers flying away. I never knew wings could be so flimsy... I should remember to not to the butt shake so enthusiastically and I must also pass on that advice as well... then no one else will have to deal with baldness... the horror.

'That will help him find you!' She smiled again. 'Do you know how long you have been here?' I shook my head.

'Well, let's say, one day here is a year.' I looked at her. 'Yep. But those feathers that just came loose, Steyvan will see them and come and find you... He's one of the few angels with tracking senses and good sense of direction without whacking into walls...' I stifled a laugh. 'Don't worry. It is pretty funny. Anyways, I shall leave you to it, you seem very content here.'

'I am, thank you, Taylor.' I plucked a flower from the ground and gave it to her. 'Can you see it? It's white, but with black spots.' She nodded. 'Can you give this to Steyvan, if you see him?' She nodded. 'Thank you.'

'Any time... I shall see you around, George.'

'And you, Taylor.' She waved bye and walked away. When she was finally gone, I started panicking. 'Oh God. If I have been here a year this time?! What's happening?!'

***

I woke up the next day in the garden, holding my head. 'Must've passed out...' I heard a few voices, none of them

Steyvan's. 'God, if you are real, and you do run this place, please lead him to me... I can't do this much longer.' I looked around to see a pond had formed with black and white swans. I took off my boots and put my feet in it for a moment. 'That's good.' I took my feet out, dried them off with the handy towel that came with the pond and started pacing again. 'Steyvan?! Where are you? I am alone and I am so scared...' After what felt like years, I sat on the floor and hugged my knees.

'George?' I heard Steyvan's voice say worriedly. I picked up my head to see him knelt in front of me.

'Steyvan!'

***

Dear diary

I thought I'd carry on my dad's tradition of keeping a diary.

Just a bit about me so you know I'm not my father.

My name is Johnathan Steyvan William Vaughn-Ray and I am 22 and due to be a father to a baby boy... or two! I am a jack of all trades, though, master of none. Sadly. I'm a master of a few! Paperwork, playing guitar like Tony Iommi and... well... I'm stupid. Haha!!

My father has been dead for a while now. It has been a tough ride but, needs must!

Anyways, I best go and check on my girlfriend, Eleanora. She's calling for food! Her cravings are RIDICULOUS! Fucking chicken soup with bacon bits. ERUGH! 'Excuse me while I go back.

Speak later!

Johnathan.
Xx

***

Chapter 1
Steyvan POV

I sat there, on my white fluffy cloud, covered in a silver silky blanket with white feathered angel wings covering me. I heard a familiar, shy, German male voice talking to himself. 'Jansn?'

'Yeah, Steyvan! It's me!' I heard his shoes clink on the marble floor of the house. 'I have alcohol and flowers!'

'Will be down in a second! Just relaxing.' I got down from my fluffy cloud I called my bed and got dressed into my white suit and tie that I was buried and got married in. I got downstairs and stroked my little white husky puppy. 'Hello, Jansn!'

'Heya, bro! I thought you would like these,' he said, pulling out a bottle of rose wine and a bunch of white roses.

'Oh, you read my mind! Crack it open then!' I said, pulling out two fluted champagne glasses from the side of the kitchen.

'We so need to catch up!' Jansn said to me with a smile.

'Well, pour that wine, and we will do!'

***

After a while, Jansn had to leave to go see his partner. Meanwhile, I took a walk. I walked down small bright alleyways, talking to people as I went along. I have been so lonely up here. I just hope George is okay... I miss him. I sat down on a white marble bench and played about with a black feather I found in my suit pocket. 'Heh... Our wedding night...' I looked up and saw similar but longer black feathers fluttering about as if a dark angel was rushing around collecting souls. 'What?'

'Steyvan?! Where are you? I am alone and I am so scared!' I heard a very faint, familiar, German-accented voice yell.

'What the—?' I followed the voice to a pretty large, black and white rose flower filled garden with a pond and a man with long black hair in a black suit with ombré black and white wings. 'Hello?' The man turned around to reveal a Goth look. 'George?! Sweetheart!'

'Steyvan. I was so lost and scared...' I hugged him, being careful of his very unique wings. 'I have missed you so much, Oh my word...'

'I've missed you too... And what's wrong?' I said, letting my wings fold up behind me.

'What I did to get here and how I did it, and these fucking wings!' George said, looking at his elegant and unique wings.

'Come to my home, get a drink and some food... You are shaking, love... How long have you been here?! Oh... and I think you lost some feathers. But I also found this in my pocket.' I pulled out the black feather and put it in his hand as he smiled slightly. He put it in his pocket as his face went all scared again.

'I don't know... I think I have just got here, but it feels like an eternity... Especially being lost! Everything looks the damn same!' I bought him into a hug, letting my wings cover him for comfort.

'Come to my home, explain everything to me, okay? You live with me. Don't worry... You are safe now.' He dug his head into my chest as I smiled. 'Come on then, George... You deserve a stiff drink.'

***

'So... When did you pass?' I asked George who sat down flinching as he sat on his wings. 'You get used to that. I'll teach you a few tricks. Just lift the butt up and pull them out. The seats support them quite well!' I said, sitting on a bar stool next to him pouring some whiskey in a small glass for George and I. 'But tell me what happened?'

'Well, I was 27, I got so depressed... I couldn't take it anymore. I had medication dispensed that day to me. I took them all. And I left the company to Johnny...' he said, wiping tears away from his eyes. 'What did I do to have this problem?!'

'Sweetheart, everything happens for a reason, being up here for a while has taught me that. And it must've happened to you 'cause it might've been your time... But never blame yourself. How old were you when you passed?'

'Twenty-seven... I'm now twenty-nine...'

'You've been here two years, George...' I said to him as he looked shocked and broke down in tears. 'Hey, George. Come here, sweetheart... It was a shock to me too when Jansn told me.' I wrapped my wings around him and my arms to give him a sense of comfort. 'Cry it out, George... We will go get lunch soon. I love your wings!'

'They are so annoying.'

'But beautiful and unique. George...' I unwrapped my wings and held him at arm's length. 'You are beautiful... Don't worry, okay? You are here now. That's all that matters.'

***

After the huge catch up and laughs, I took George to meet Jansn. 'Jansn?! It's me! Steyvan!'

'Okay! Just feeding the dog!'

'Jansn is here?!' George asked me as I nodded. 'What does he look like?' A tall man with blonde hair and a friendly smile in white top and trousers came through. 'Jansn!' George ran up to Jansn and hugged him. 'Careful of the wings!'

'He's not got used to them yet,' I said to Jansn, laughing slightly.

'Sorry, bro. Wow, you look healthy!'

'As do you, Jansn! I've been living off the fruits in the garden for God knows...'

'Let's all catch up! WITH SPIN THE BOTTLE! What ya say, bro?!'

'I say you are so gay, it's fabulous. LET'S DO IT!' George said with a huge smile.

***

The next morning, I woke up bright and early. Bought a ring etc. 'Hey, George… Will you marry me? As my angelic husband?' I asked him. He said yes as I smiled and stroked his angelic ombré wings… Days later, we were married! 'I have missed you so much, George!'

'Let's just have a fun day…'

***

Dear Diary.

Johnny here, again.

Two deaths in one week. Luckily, I know protocol. Shut off the area, phone up the family, the undertakers, blah blah blah. It's a simple thing.

Eleanora is looking after the baby. He is so precious! Steyvan William Vaughn-Ray the Third… Well, he is a Vaughn-Ray by blood after all!!!!

I best get to work. There is a HUGE heat wave and the AC decided to break! NOT A GOOD TIME!

Be back soon!

Johnathan
xx

***

Chapter 2
George POV

I looked into a small fountain and an image appeared. 'Johnny…' I carried on watching just like when I binged *Desperate Housewives* just a day earlier. I saw my son hugging a little two-year-old son. *"Heya, lil' Steyvan!"* I gasped as Johnny looked up. 'I left my son… He had a child… God! What did I do?'

'Excuse me… Are you okay?' I heard from a very shy female voice behind me.

'Sorry… I'm fine… sorry. Um… just had a scare is all.' I turned around to see a woman with long blonde hair and pure white wings with one red feather. 'Sorry. I can be a bit paranoid.'

'Bless you! I saw your wings and wondered if everything was okay? I just watched you for a bit looking into the fountain, body language looked worried… I'm Rose.'

'George… And my wings are always like this.'

'You are Steyvan's partner?! I talk to him every day! I have heard so much about you! He told me to look out for you but not act like a creep.'

'I am. And it's fine.' I sat down on the fountains wall as she joined me. Her white dress flowed and complimented her movements.

'There is a rumour about this fountain… but I don't know if it is true or not.' I looked at her intrigued. 'Let's go for a cuppa. I will tell you then.'

***

I followed Rose to a little cafe like place. We sat down and ordered some coffee. 'So, why did you ask about my wings?' I asked Rose who sipped her Americano.

'Wings change with our moods! Though, it does depend on the originality of the wings too. Yours are beautiful. But that fountain has a rumour.' I listened intently as I picked up my large latte. 'Rumour has it, that if you put a penny in the fountain or even step into the fountain, it takes you to what you want most. You will be your actual age and everything but alive. And well. And another rumour has it, immortal.' I put down my cup in shock.

'You what?' She nodded. 'So, if I say, put an euro in it and wish to be with Steyvan, alive again, it could do that?' Rose nodded. 'Wow…'

'Don't do anything stupid.' I shook my head. 'Let's go find Steyvan. Get you back home.'

***

'You okay, Steyvan?' I looked over to see him asleep like old times. 'Sweet.' I crawled into the fluffy cloud and snuggled up to my literal angelic husband. His right wing covered me as I felt more comfortable. I stroked his beautiful, pure, crystal white wings as I slowly fell into a deep sleep.

***

I felt my body being picked up gently, one by my arms, one by my legs. I opened by eyed to Steyvan gone from next to me, then up to see Taylor and Rose carrying me. I couldn't speak. It was as if someone had put a spell on my voice to mute me. No matter how much I tried screaming, not a single sound came out. *Please… No…* I mouthed to the two-winged women carrying me. *Where's Steyvan?*

'He's safe… shh…' Taylor replied before somehow making my body somewhat lifeless apart from my eyes.

No… No… I thought as I saw what I named the *Fountain of Life* in my sights. As my anxiety and fright rose, I grunted and tried to wiggle out of Rose and Taylors grip… But it was impossible.

'I've had enough of this.' I heard Taylor say. 'It's for the best that I do this George. She waved her hand in front of my face and put me into a comatose like state. 'On three Rose?'

'On three! One, two… three!' Rise yelled as they chucked me into the fountain. What they did not realise, all spells casted were erased when I hit the water.

'No!' I screamed out. Next thing I knew, I was in darkness

***

I felt my body fall as if I jumped off a cliff. I landed on something which woke me up. 'What the—?!' I woke up and looked next to me to see Steyvan asleep. 'Steyvan, wake up. Punch me.' He looked at me and whacked me in a place that shouldn't be whacked. 'ANYWHERE APART FROM MY BALLS, ASSHOLE! But it is real.'

'What's fucking real?' Steyvan said, sitting up. 'What the?' I got up and opened the door to see Johnny cradling a little boy. I gasped and closed the door before he saw me. 'What?' I pointed to the door as Steyvan wrapped a blanket around him to keep his dignity and he opened the door. 'Shit!'

'Keep it the fuck down!' I whispered. 'He doesn't know!'

'What in the world? Lil' Steyvan?' I heard our son say. I grabbed Steyvan and ran into the bathroom. I heard the door open. 'What in the world?' I peeked through the keyhole to see Johnny looking around the room. 'I must be imagining things. Swear I just heard Dad… oh well!' He walked out the room.

'Told you to keep it down!' I said, slapping Steyvan as I exited the bathroom. I looked at the window. 'Let me deal with this.' I grabbed some clothes and my platform boots. I put it all on and started pacing the room.

'Okay…' Steyvan stared at me. 'So, how about you, go out, hug him, say nothing.' I nodded. 'Do it, now. I'm starving and so thirsty.'

'I'm going!' I put on a bit of my signature Goth makeup but just the heavy black eyeliner and black lips. 'Do I look okay?'

'For someone that's been dead nearly three years, you're hot as fuck,' Steyvan relayed to me with a wink.

'Thanks!' I replied with a hint of sarcasm. 'Let's do this.' I opened the door and saw Johnny down the hallway holding a 2-year-old little boy while talking to a client. I went up to him, quietly, and hugged him. 'Hello, son,' I said to him as he looked at me.

'Give it up, Uncle Dodi. It's not funny.'

'Johnny. It's me…' I took his hand as the client went into his room. 'Come with me.' I walked back up the white hallway and knocked on the door of where Steyvan was. 'You decent?' I peeked into the door to see Steyvan nod. 'Come on, Johnathan.' I led him into the bedroom where Steyvan sat on the bed. 'You okay?'

'What the fuck?' I heard Johnny say as he looked at Steyvan. 'Dad!'

'We don't know ourselves, Johnny… Who's this little one?!' Steyvan asked, taking the child from Johnny.

'My son, Steyvan William George Vaughn-Ray,' Johnny said as Steyvan shed a small tear. 'After you two… So, how will we deal with this?'

'No idea… But he is so precious!' Steyvan said, smiling away. 'Hello, lil' man!'

'I think you lost your child, Johnny.' I looked at Steyvan and smiled. 'But Steyvan said he's hungry and tired. Cafe?'

***

'Oh my word, this has improved!' Steyvan said, eating a piled plate of bacon, eggs and sausages. 'Oh my God, this is nice!'

'I just wanted a bacon butty…' I said, smiling. 'He wanted the whole fucking buffet!' Johnny laughed as he fed his son. 'Bless him! He is so adorable… Looks like you and Eleanora! Talking of Eleanora, how is she?'

'She's fine, pregnant again, but fine.'

'OH MY GOD! CONGRATULATIONS!' I said to him surprised. 'Bless you! What is it?'

'A girl, we think.' I smiled. 'Anyways, I best go, come on lil' man!' Johnny picked up his son to put him on his hip. 'Let's get you down for a nap and me to paperwork. Your ID cards and keys are on your desk, Daddy G.'

'Thanks,' I said, looking to Steyvan, who was stuffing his face. 'I'll be back, babe... Need to find Marilyn. I kissed him gently on the cheek and smiled. I walked out of the cafe and went to an office door that had "Marilyn 'Blobby' Jamie-Robinson" on it. I knocked.

'Come in.' I heard an English, gay as anything, voice say. I walked in and closed the door. 'Take a seat, I will be with you in a moment.' He looked at his screen and carried on typing. When he finished, he looked up as his face went into shock. 'What?! George! Oh my word!' He hugged me and kissed my cheeks one on each side. 'Wow! You look... dead. Literally.'

'I have no idea how I am back, but I fucking know for sure I have missed your gayer than a pink-fart ass,' I hugged him and smiled. 'So, Looks like you have been working hard! Swanky new office!'

'Made it as gay as me, lovely,' he smiled at me and took off his glasses. 'Is he back?' I nodded. 'Tell him to come in. I miss him.'

'I will do! You up for a drink tonight?' He sat there and threw me a look as I got up. 'Stupid question!'

'Well! DUH! A girl needs a night out. Haha! See you later, Mother Mothra.' He looked at me as I pretended my trench coat I slipped on just moments ago were wings.

'MOTHER MOTHRA, OUT!'

***

'Well! That was a great night!' I said to Steyvan who had a peppermint green and white night top on. 'I used that when you were gone,' I announced, giggling.

'Well, after all we drunk tonight, we should sleep. Love you, George.' He snuggled into my chest as I half-expected his wings to go around me. But I only then remembered, we are human, until his wings did go around me. 'We keep our wings... but not visible to the human eye unless we make them...'

***

Dear Diary

That was a surprise! To see my fathers are back! Wonder how it happened. But, it's not a need to know. Just glad they are back!

Anyways, it has been a long day for me and I'm drunk. So. Good night!

Johnathan
Xx

Chapter 3
Johnny POV

I woke up and picked up my son from his bed. 'Good morning!' he smiled at me. 'You going to try copy, Daddy?'

'Potty time!' he said to me smiling. 'BIG BOY TOILET!'

'We can try, Steyvan! Just hold onto me!' I said, laughing. 'I love you, son. What do you want? A brother or a sister?!' I asked him as Eleanora came out of the bedroom, bump bigger than ever.

'A SISTER!'

'Well, my little one,' Eleanora said to Steyvan. 'You will be having a baby sister!' Our son smiled and cried happy tears. 'Bless you! Now, Daddy's going to toilet train you, okay? Mummy is going to go shopping. She needs a few bits.' I stroked Steyvan's hair as he smiled. 'See you later, babbs,' Eleanora said before kissing me.

'See you soon. Love you!' Eleanora blew a kiss and I caught it and smushed my hand against my son's face. 'Ewww! You have Mummy's kissy germs all over you!' I said, laughing. 'Come on then, lil' dude! Let's get you started!'

***

After a successful session, both happened. 'THAT'S MY MAN!' I said, high-fiving him after he washed his hands. 'You are doing so, so well! Let's see what Daddy has as a reward!' He walked next to me at his own pace to go to the staff room. We finally got there and I went into a bag and gasped. 'Oh! Daddy has got something special for you!' I bought out a medium-sized teddy in the shape of a giraffe. 'The Toilet Fairy knew you liked giraffes and asked me to give this to you!' I gave it to him as he smiled and hugged the giraffe. 'Bless. Go on then, matey! Daddy's going to work. Just over there!' I pointed to the desk right near him. 'Mummy is in bed, okay? She's not that well.' I kissed the top of his head and sat down at my mahogany wood desk. I looked at the photos of me and my fathers and a photo of Eleanora and I when our son was born. 'Okay. Let's get on.'

***

After an hour, I looked up to see my parents sat at their own desks and then my son asleep on the floor cuddling to his teddy. 'Bless… I'll get him to bed.' I picked him up gently as Daddy S put the giraffe onto my son's body who just grasped it with his hands. I walked to his room, put him in his bed and covered him. As I walked out, I gently closed the door and looked in on Eleanora. 'Bless.' She was sound asleep and cuddling up to the quilt. I slowly and quietly closed the door and walked back to the office. 'Daddy G?' I asked as I sat back down in my chair.

'Yes, sprog?' My father, well, mother, said in his German accent looking through his glasses.

'Look at this,' I motioned him over to show him an elegant, pink sapphire engagement ring. 'What do you think? Or another colour?'

'Is that one her favourite? If so how much of that does she wear?'

'Too much.'

'Try blue. Match her eyes. Why though?'

'Never thought of that! Thanks!' I pointed to a blue one. 'That one? It's gold, blue sapphire and pink sapphire? And I'm going to ask her!'

'Perfect! And OH MY GOD THAT'S SO SWEET!' My father gave me his card and smiled. 'Hey, a dad wants to help his son get the perfect wedding!'

'Dad… You sure?' He nodded. 'No arguments?' He nodded and took off his glasses. 'Okay.' I pressed pay on the HM Samuels website and put in the details and pressed confirm. 'Tomorrow! Thank you so much, Dad…'

'Johnny. Don't need to thank me,' my father smiled. 'As I have said. I don't want you to have the same life that I had. I don't want you to go to drugs and that… I want your life to be perfect. I want you to have a great family. Eight kids and twenty dogs and cats. If that is what makes you and your family happy, that is all I care about.' I felt my father's forehead and cheek.

'Well, you're not ill.' My father's and I started to have a laugh. 'Dad, thank you so much… I love you, Dad. I hope you know that.'

'I love you too, Johnny.' My father walked to his desk and sat down. 'How old is your little one?'

'Two.' I smiled, turning my attention towards my computer. 'Best wake up Ella, have I not?'

'Yeah, bless her!' I heard Daddy S say. 'See you in a few!'

***

'Ella…' I said as I entered the bedroom. 'Wake up sweetheart! Steyvan's asleep.'

'I didn't mean to fall asleep… Sorry, Johnny…'

'It's fine… You need it. Come on… Let's go outside…' I took her hand and arm to help her out of bed.

'Thanks…' She looked at me as her fragile yet graceful smile fell. 'You okay?' I nodded. 'You seem troubled.'

'I'm fine, Ella… Just tired, I think. Been staring at a screen all day!' I smiled. 'Come on then.'

***

The next day soon came as did the ring. I opened the box to reveal an elegant and sparkling ring with one pink sapphire and one blue sapphire and showed it to my fathers. 'Oh, My GOD! THAT IS BEAUTIFUL!' they said in unison.

'I'm ready…' My father's shoved me out of the office and locked the door and did the "Go on then!" look. I saw Eleanora sat on the sofa by the front entrance. I closed the box and smiled. 'Hey Ella…' I walked over to her and knelt on the floor. 'Heya, little one…' I kissed her bump and smiled. I got back up and sat next to her. 'How you feeling?'

'Better thanks…' she smiled and sipped some milk. 'Milk's helping.' I put my hand through her long, blonde, freshly curled hair. 'Johnny?'

'Ella…' I handed her the box and smiled sheepishly. 'Open it… It kind of speaks for itself.'

'Okay…' She opened the box and looked up with a surprised look. 'What?'

'Ella… Will you marry me?'

***

Dear Diary
    Ella said yes!! I'm going to spend time with her…

    Good night

Johnathan.

Chapter 4
Marilyn POV

'Hello! It's Maz!' I said into the intercom to my "friend's" flat.

'Oh! Hey, Maz! I'll let you in! Number twenty-two!' A male voice said coming out of the speaker as I took off my sparkly sequin blazer. I walked up four flights of stairs and down a hallway to be faced with a black door with the number twenty-two on the front written in a unique font. All of a sudden, the door opened to reveal a tall male wearing a pair of black shorts. 'MAZ!' he yelled with excitement as he greeted me. 'In!' I walked in and looked around. A lovely modern black and white apartment greeted me. 'What brings you to my new humble abode? You okay?' I shook his head as he made a coffee for the both of us. 'What's up, Marilyn? You are not the usual gay as a pink-fart fluff cloud that you usually are!'

'I don't know what to do right now, Adam,' I said, walking to the window to look over the Parisian landscape with the Eiffel tower in my view. 'I came back home to talk to you... about that...' I went to sit on the luxurious black sofa and sighed. 'Okay... George has offered you a place, with me. Do you want it?' He nodded and looked at me with excitement. 'Okay... Second of all, Adam... Will you be mine?'

'Yes!!!' he said happily in his sweet French accent.

'Oh... Okay. I'll just—hang on. Did you just say yes?' Adam nodded and smiled. 'Wow... I've tried to get a boyfriend for ages... No one would take me... Wow...'

'God, MAZ! SNAP OUT OF IT, DARLING!' Adam said to me bringing me into a massive hug. 'You are you. That is why I love you.' I smiled as I grabbed my bag when he let go of the hug. 'What are you doing?' he asked as his face fell from a happy smile to a slight frown.

'Get your bag ready. You are going to England.'

***

'Whoa dude! This building is... IMMENSE!' Adam said to me as I grabbed out my ID and lanyard.

'Just... Keep your cool, Adam. George will be here soon.' Adam nodded as the glass doors opened and I led him through to my office. 'Sorry about the decor... I just like to keep a few keepsakes in here...' I said, putting picture frames face down of memories of my son and daughter. 'Also a few weird bits... Sorry.' I put more things into my desk drawers and smiled. 'Anyways. Yeah, just be prepared for George.'

'Keep them out, Maz... Don't worry... and okay, what does he look like and that?' Adam asked me, intrigued.

'He is Goth, long black hair etc. Generally, with Steyvan,' I sighed and sat in my chair after dumping my bag in the corner of the room.

'Okay... You okay, Maz?' I picked up a frame and rubbed my thumb against the picture.

'I... I'm fine, Adam... Just a bit emotional right now. I'm a whole wreck...' I heard a knock on the door and quickly got my composure. 'Come in!' I logged onto my computer as George stuck his head in. His hair drooped down and his eyes sparkled. 'George, this is Adam. Boyfriend and new employee of yours.'

'Awesome! I need to borrow Blobby for a few, I will deal with you in a few, Maz! My office!' he squealed with delight.

'Okay...' I walked out of my office and closed the door. 'What's up?'

'Come with me!' He led me to the disabled staff toilets. 'Well. Ready?' I nodded and looked at him intrigued. He took off his top and turned around to me to show me a back tattoo of angel wings. 'What ya think?!'

'FUCK ME! Didn't that hurt?!' He shook his head. 'Love it though!'

'Fuck yeah! Anyways, you look sad. Speak to me.' He put on his top again and made himself look smart. 'Is it about what happened?' I nodded as I started to cry. 'Hey... Marilyn... She's not in pain anymore, okay? That's all you need to think of. She is no longer in pain...' He took me into his arms and rocked me back and forth. 'Want me to go deal with Adam while you tidy yourself up and cry it out?' I nodded and sniffled. 'Okay... I'll be back. I'll say you went for a nap.'

'Okay... See you in a few.' I sniffled again as he left the toilet. I locked the door and collapsed as if I had no spine, right against the door in a fit of tears.

***

I heard a knock at the door 10 minutes later. I unlocked the door and opened it to see Steyvan standing there. 'George sent me to see if you were okay...' He came into the toilet and locked the door. 'Hang on...' He sat opposite me, holding something in his coat. 'Thought this lil' guy would cheer you up. Be careful though... He was born about six weeks ago, okay?' I nodded as he took out the thing he was holding. A six-week-old chocolate Labrador puppy.

'Oh my word... You serious? I know how much your litters mean to you!' He nodded as he handed me the pup. 'Hello, pupper... I might name you... Autumn.'

'Suits him!' Steyvan said, smiling. 'You coming back into your office?' I nodded, wiping the last of my tears away, wiping off the streaked makeup while holding the puppy. 'If you need help with him, let me know and I will help.'

'Thank you so much, Steyvan...' He smiled. 'He's so cute!' He whimpered as I adjusted the hold I had him in. Steyvan helped me by adjusting my hand.

'Tip. Three fingers in between his legs and one on each outside of his legs. It's a bit more comfy makes them feel like they are lying on something soft when you do that hold!' I smiled as he looked at me. 'Enjoy, okay?' I nodded again as I walked out of the toilet and to my office. I put the puppy on the desk. 'I'll come back with a lead and collar for him! Want pink?'

'Oh! Please! That would look lovely!' I exclaimed. 'When is walkies?'

'Put puppy pads everywhere, and when I comeback with the collar and lead, I will help you with that. He is a feisty one.'

'Okay… Thank you so, so much!'

'No problem!' Steyvan said to me, walking out and closing the door behind him.

'You are precious…'

***

'Maz!' I heard George yell from his office. 'You been on a spending spree again?' I walked to his office and I nodded. 'What on?'

'We needed to updated logic on the Macs and Macbooks,' I said, hugging Autumn. 'So I thought I'd do it for you! I was JUST about to tell you. Cause I JUST did it.'

'Oh yeah, we did. Duh. Numbnuts. Thanks for that, Marilyn! I was going to do it but forgot.'

'It's cool,' I smiled. 'How you feeling?'

'Fine… How's Adam settling in?' George asked as he took off his glasses. 'Also, have you seen Johnathan?'

'I have, actually. Johnny is with Eleanora, who's really got bad sickness and Adam is settling in really well, thanks.' I put down Autumn as she whined a little bit. 'Autumn. Come here, girl!' I sat on the floor and stroked his ears. 'Good boy…'

'Poor Ella… When is she due?' George asked, sitting down with me.

'Any day now…' I put my head on his shoulder as he gave Autumn some attention. 'Where's Steyvan?'

'Out getting food,' I sniggered. 'Cooks fucked off again.'

'Get a new chef?' He shook his head.

'So… Did you name him Autumn after… you know?' I nodded. 'Is that why you were really upset?' I nodded again. 'Bless you… Come here…' George put his arms around me. 'You can't help life, sweetheart… If it helps, I know a few surrogates?'

'No… no… Me and Adam are on about adopting anyways.'

'Sweet… Boy or girl?'

'Boy… Then a girl so he has someone to defend,' I said as the office door opened. 'Hey, Steyvan.' Steyvan sauntered in like he owns the place, wait, he does, and passed me a pink collar and a pink lead.

'There you go! Vets are coming around to do her jabs soon,' Steyvan said as I picked up the collar and smiled.

'Awesome!' I looked at the collar. It was baby pink with silver bones on it. Same as the lead. 'Autumn! Come here, boy!' The little adorable chocolate Labrador puppy bounded over and placed his neck in the right position for me to slip on the collar. 'Good boy!' I did it up to the right size. Enough for him to move, eat and drink with ease. I scratched his ear and smiled. 'Good boy!'

'Glad you like him!' Steyvan said, sitting down. 'Now, skedaddle, Marilyn. I need time with George.'

***

'Good morning… You okay, Adam?' Adam nodded. 'Having a mute day?' He nodded again. 'Okay… I will let George know… He knows sign language. It will be okay.' I swung my legs out of bed. 'It's a girly day!'

***

'Good m—what?' I said, walking into Johnny's room. Eleanora lay there, cradling a newborn baby girl in her arms, umbilical cord still attached. 'Oh wow! Congratulations! Where's Dad?' Eleanora pointed to the floor. 'Passed out?' She nodded as she went to reach for a towel. 'Hang on.' She revealed her breast and started feeding the little girl. 'What you going to name her?' I passed a towel to the messy and bedraggled-looking Eleanora. She slightly covered herself up for a bit of modesty.

'Janine Autumn Marilyn. After your little girl.' I smiled and let a small tear sneak out. 'She helped Johnny get over a lot… It's the least we could do.' I saw Johnny get up, look at the baby and pass out again. 'He did this with Steyvan!' she said, laughing. 'He'll be fine after this one.' I laughed as she caressed her baby's head. 'Can you do me a favour?' I looked at her. 'Unhook me and get this fucking placenta out!'

'Whoa! Calm down! I will do! When you have finished feeding, I'll take her to see George or drag him in here.' I did what she asked me to, quickly, professionally and cleanly. 'There you go… Want to eat some?' She made a hacking noise as I laughed.

'Drag him in.' I nodded. 'How are you?'

'Good… What about you, Eleanora?' I said, texting George to come into the room. 'And he shouldn't be long.'

'Awesome, and I've just given birth. How do you think I fucking feel?' I looked at her and laughing. Johnny poked his head up again. 'Morning, Johnny! Nice nap?' Eleanora said with sarcasm.

'Oh, shut it.' Johnny said, hoisting himself onto the bed.

'Knock, knock!' George said, walking through the door. 'He passed out again?' Eleanora nodded. 'Let's have a look then!'

'I'll leave you all to it.' I walked out of the room and grabbed my car keys from my back pocket. 'Yo, Adam! Get in the car!' I walked over to a black Jaguar sports car. 'We are going for a ride.'

***

A few days later, I woke up and went to see George who was sat in his office at 2 am. 'George?'

'Maz? What the fuck are you doing up?' he asked me, taking off his glasses. 'You okay?'

'Just… Needed a chat and saw your office light on… hope you don't mind.' He pointed to the seat in front of him. 'Why you still up?'

'Trying to do some paperwork, head's not working… Why are you up though, Maz? That's more important. Want a ciggy and a chat about it?'

***

Dear Diary
  I'm a father! More soon!!

  Good night

Johnny
Xxx

***

Chapter 5
George POV

George, STOP! You cannot relapse or show your emotions!
'Hey, Maz. Come on. We will talk it out.'

'Okay.' I stepped outside of the office, Marilyn in tow. Cigarette in our hands, lighter too. 'It's this Autumn thing… I'm really depressed…'

'As I said, Marilyn, you couldn't have done anything… It was her time.' I wiped Marilyn's tears away and put his head close to my chest. 'Hey, Maz, calm down, okay?'

'Sorry, George… I'm acting like a complete blubbering idiot.'

'That is why I'm here.' I held him at arm's length. 'Okay. How about, we go to a bar, get drunk and talk it out. Or even better, my room, vodka. You bring the glasses.' He nodded and smiled. 'Okay…'

'Where's Steyvan?' I shrugged as I put my cigarette out and blew out the rest of the smoke. 'I am also surprised your lungs ain't done in with all that smoking.'

'I've cut down a LOT, Maz.' I looked into his deep-sea blue eyes. 'Like I'm at about two packs a day cut down.' I smiled as his hair hid his eyes slightly after the wind blew. 'Anyways, let's go in…' I smiled and walked inside.

***

'Oh, George!' I heard from the door of my office and a simple French accent. 'It's me! Maz!'

'Come in, Maz! It's only me!' I said as Marilyn walked in looking like Marilyn Monroe in the signature white halterneck dress with petticoat and curled hair. 'Whoa! Hello Miss Monroe!' I look off my glasses and winked. 'Voddy and alcohol is in the draw!' I said as Marilyn put down the glasses for the drinks. 'I would not say no.'

'Well, what if I offered my body now?' Marilyn asked me, pouring out the drinks.

'I'd get naked now. Oh yes… I would say yes.'

'Well. Let's get a little drunk, and I may just offer you that,' he said with a wink.

'Deal!'

***

I woke up and saw Marilyn lying next to me, his bare skin touching mine. 'Maz?'

'Huh? Morning, George. What time is it?'

'Four am. But what happened?!'

'I'm your boyfriend.' I slammed my palm against my face. 'I'm going back to sleep.'

'Okay… I'm going to get up,' I smiled as he rolled over to go back to sleep. I got out of bed and did my normal routine. Hair, teeth etc. The norm. I got breakfast and a drink for the day. I walked into my office, just in shorts and turned on my computer to see four emails. 'Steyvan?'

Email me back as soon as you get this!
Steyvan xxx

'Oh fuck.'

You usually answer quick! Please email me!
Steyvan xxx

'What the?'

GEORGE!!! I NEED TO TALK ASA-FUCKING-P!!!
Steyvan xxx

'I think I best email him!'

Please answer… I am so worried now, babe… Please?
Steyvan xxx

'Okay then. Time to get my head blown off.' I clicked to reply as a new email came through.

George… Please…

'Okay. Let's do this.' I clicked the email that I was about to write and started typing my heart out.

Steyvan,

I am so, so sorry I did not get back in touch. Something happened that I think you should know about. I... Oh my giddy aunt. I... I had sex with Maz. I didn't mean for this to happen! We got drunk, he was playing dress up, I am so, so sorry, Steyvan. Please forgive me. I'll never leave your side... We maybe fallen angels, but love endurance stretches... I didn't mean it. I am so sorry.

Also, about the emails, sorry about that... I've been so busy doing paperwork. What's up your end? Dodi has joined us, Adam has, Odette, not yet. Well. I best get on with work! See you soon

> *Luff ya like a muffa!*
> *The Goth xxx*
> *George Vaughn-Ray*
> *Owner*
> *Vaughn-Ray LTD.*
> *Grantham*
> *Lincs*
> *England.*
> *Fax 01476 555909*
> *Tel. 07890123666*

'Just hope he accepts the apology.' I bought up iTunes to put on some classical calming music to calm my nerves. I then started to file all my paperwork into the files as I heard the dreaded Email notification that I had set for Steyvan's emails. 'Oh no…'

George

I forgive you! Everything happens for one reason or another. And about the emails, don't worry your lil' black lippy off! It's just you usually answer within seconds. Everything is going well! How is the company going that side of the ocean? Here, we have a 70-room building! That is just rooms for the clientele! Don't get me started on everything else!! Anyways. Get on with work. See you soon.

Steyvan xxx

I breathed a sigh of relief as I read that email. 'Okay... let's get to work.'

***

Dear Diary
Johnny here!
So tired today! There again, new baby and all! Dad is asleep now... He needs it.
Gonna go to bed myself! I'm knackered!! Done so much paperwork and... nappy changing. ERUGH! THEY SMELT TO HIGH HEAVEN!! Actually... what DOES heaven smell like? I'll ask my fathers tomorrow.
Never thought I'd say that!
Good night

Johnny, Ella and the sprogs xx

***

Chapter 6
Johnny POV

'My life is a mess…' I said with frustration as I was looking for some important paperwork. I found my passport and smiled. 'Well. Found one bit.' I saw Dad come in with his cases. 'Ready, Dad?' I asked my Gothic, long, black-haired father.

'YES!' he giggled. 'Just wait till you see your grandmother!' I heard a squeal coming from down the hallway as a Geisha walked in. 'Aunt Coco, what's going on?!'

'She excited. Sorry. Me said nothing!' I laughed as she tripped over her own feet as my father and I caught her. 'Hehe! Sorry… Me excited too! Get to see onee-saan and Okiya!'

'Well, Aunt Coco Pops, please calm down!' I said, straightening her up. 'Anyways, everyone ready?' My father nodded as my other father, Steyvan, ran past me. 'The kids are in the car already and asleep with Ella.'

'Good!' my Gothic father said with excitement. 'LET'S GO!'

***

'You okay, lil' man?' I asked my 6-year-old son, who sat beside me on the plane just watching the world go by. 'Want a drink?' He shook his head. 'What's up, mate?'

'I miss Mummy…' I put an arm around him. 'She's with Elsie, ain't she?'

'She is, matey… She's okay though! I just went to see if she was okay, and she is fine.' I bought him into a hug so he knew I was there.

'We will soon be landing. Please put seatbelts on,' the pilot announced. I put my seatbelt and my son's and smiled. After a rough landing, the pilot announced something again. 'You may undo your seatbelts, get luggage and enjoy Tokyo, Japan!'

'OH MY FOX GOD!' I heard my grandmother squeal again.

'Well, she found out, son!' My Gothic, no-makeuped, father said.

'Ah balls. Oh well!'

***

We eventually got to Kyoto, where, sadly, lots of things have happened in the past. We sat in a traditional Japanese Geisha-run tea house where my grandmother's aunt worked. I saw a man with one of them. He was tall, slender and wearing a black suit to match his black tie and accessories. 'Johnny, this is my Danna-Sama, Chōei,' my aunt Kiyomi said to me in full Geisha attire. She walked over gracefully and bowed.

'Ohayō gozaimasu. Nice to meet you, sir,' I said to Chōei as I bowed in the traditional male Japanese way. 'I am Johnny, this is my son, Steyvan, my daughter, Elsie and wife, Eleanora.' Steyvan, my son, bowed as did Eleanora, but in the traditional female way. My daughter, Elsie, lay there fast asleep in her travel seat.

'Nice to meet you too, Johnny.' He knelt down next to us, Aunt Kiyomi followed in the traditional Geisha way. 'I have heard a lot about you.'

'What is a Danna-Sama, Chōei?'

'I am basically your divine Geisha aunt's husband. Not marriage husband, but that is what we are classed as.' I smiled as four other Geishas served tea to people in the art of Tea Ceremony, also known as The Way of the Tea. Everyone fell quiet as this happened. Eleanora, Steyvan, my father's and I watched in Awe at what they did with their delicate, precise hands. The tea was precisely and exactly made and tasted to make sure it was okay for us to drink. *This is just... Fascinating...* I thought, watching on the Geishas, who quickly finished what they did. As soon as the ceremony was over, people started talking again. 'This is what happens all the time in Japan, my dear Johnny,' Chōei said to me smiling. 'You do get used to being waited on hand and foot by these elegant women.' He stroked Kiyomi's chin who smiled, as she had to. 'I give this one money, that is basically my role. Shower her in lavish kimonos, robes, hair ornaments and more.'

'That is actually really cool,' I said, amazed. Chōei laughed.

'That it is, Johnny. Kiyomi, get us some of that lovely adult drink please? I shall get you that kimono that the Okiya won't.' Chōei winked at Aunt Kiyomi as he caressed her chin. She bowed like a Geisha. Hands on the floor, not too far apart, not too close together. 'Thank you.'

'So, how is life in Japan?' I asked Chōei politely.

'Tomorrow, I shall show you and your family, with the company of Kiyomi and a few other Geisha and Maiko, around the province. For now, wet your lips with this wondrous alcoholic drink. Would you care for some, Mrs Eleanora?'

'I shan't. Sorry, Chōei, I have baby to feed,' Eleanora smiled. 'Thank you anyway.'

'No worries, Eleanora. Baby is more important. Maybe another time,' Chōei said to my wife, who smiled back, as he accepted her apology. 'Where are you all staying?'

'At the Kyomachiya Ryokan Sakura Urushitei. I hope I pronounced that right!' My father, George, said to Chōei, smiling.

'Nice choice, sir! What is your name?' Chōei asked, extending out his hand.

'George. George Vaughn-Ray. Angel, quite literally, co-owner of Vaughn-Ray LTD and married to this loving man.

Steyvan,' my father said, shaking Chōei's hand. 'Nice to meet you.' my other father, Steyvan, poked his head out and waved before turning his attention back to his book that he had in front of him. 'Don't mind him… He is very shy…'

'Ah, okay,' Chōei said as I got up.

'You will have to excuse my departure. I am very tired and lagging. Very sorry, Chōei. I also need my medication.' He nodded understandingly. 'I shall see you later, Dad. Elle… Don't worry about waking me. I will be like a rock.' I bent down to kiss her and little Elsie.

'Okay, sweetheart… See you soon.'

'Oyasumi… Good night,' I said, bowing before leaving the teahouse. I walked outside and winced a little bit as I sat down on the steps to let my legs adjust from kneeling all that time. 'That shit hurts… hope I don't need to do that much more.' I lit up a cigarette that I took out of my father's pocket and watched the world go by.

***

I walked under the cherry blossom trees as I saw blossoms fall onto the floor. 'Fallen samurais for their emperor's. Lovely sight…' I heard from behind me. I jumped as I looked to see a young lady in an elegant kimono. 'Oh. Sorry! I tend to scare people,' she sighed. 'I am Toyoko.'

'Johnny… It's fine… My children scare me all the time. I am used to it… You look beautiful, Toyoko. Are you a Maiko?' I said to her examining her kimono that trailed along the ground. She shook her head. 'What are you then?'

'A normal passer-by like you and a blossom lover! It's currently Hanami. I often sleep amongst the fallen blossoms; I saw you looking at them… Each fallen blossom signifies a samurai fallen for their emperor.' I stood there in astonishment. 'I make my own kimono.'

'That is amazing you know that! I thought no one knew that! My wife isn't very interested in that stuff… She is more fashion and that… Not history.'

'Let's walk together? We can talk about all this.'

'I need to sleep, sorry, maybe tomorrow night, Toyoko?' She nodded. 'Want me to walk you back home?'

'During Hanami, this is my home. Underneath the blossoms of April. Meet here tomorrow?' I nodded. 'Okay. See you soon, Johnny.'

'And you, Toyoko. Sayonara,' I said to her checking my phone in my bag.

'Sayonara!'

***

I finally reached the hotel room and lay on the bed. 'That is lovely.' I let my eyes droop and just drop into a sweet deep sleep.

***

Dear Diary

Met so many nice people today! That's just one great thing about this! More tomorrow!

Night!

Johnny.

***

Chapter 7
George POV

'So! That's the main part of Kyoto you need to know!' I heard Chōei say in front of us. 'Any questions?' We all shook our heads. 'Great! I shall send out a few Geishas to accompany you to the shops for translation purposes. Garcia, I understand you are fluent in Japanese?' My mother nodded and said yes in Japanese. 'Great! Well, guys! If you need me, contact me! Sayonara!'

'Will do!' I said, smiling. 'Bye, Chōei!'

***

A few hours later, we all sat around a table enjoying a Japanese traditional meal. 'This is lovely, Chōei, thank you.'

'Anytime,' our host said politely in his Japanese accent. 'Anyways, go and explore Japan after! We shall meet at the teahouse later.'

'I think I'll crash later. Jet lag and that,' my son said to all of us as he yawned.

'Fair enough, Johnny.' Chōei said as he accepted my son's decision. 'See you tomorrow.'

'Night, mate!' Steyvan said to our son. He got up and walked out. Leaving me, Chōei, Steyvan and Eleanora.

'Bless him. He really looks like the fox, God has put a curse on him!' Eleanora said to me.

'You know… The Zenko?!' Chōei said, shocked. 'What fox spirit do you connect with most?'

'Oh… Has to be… Either, Seishin, kitsune of spirit or Ongaku, the kitsune of music!' Eleanora said with enthusiasm.

'Cannot believe you know about the 13 kitsune spirits! Sit next to me! We shall talk about Shintoism!' Chōei said with pure excitement.

'Come on, Steyvan! Let's go for a walk and leave them two to it,' George, my father, said laughing.

***

Dear Diary
I don't know what to think. It's a struggling time for me…

Johnny…

***

Chapter 8
Johnny POV

I walked back to the cherry blossom trees to see Toyoko lying beneath the trees with a handmade blossom headdress and a bright pink, cherry blossom covered kimono. 'Toyoko?' I said as she turned her head and smiled. 'You okay?' I helped her up as cherry blossoms fell off her kimono, that fell onto her kimono in the first place, and put her shoes on after she was up.

'JOHNNY!' she hugged me with great force. 'Sorry.' She fluffed out her Kimono again and smiled. 'I am fine! And you?'

'I'm good. Thanks. You look elegant today!'

'Thank you... Had tea with my family,' she said through clenched teeth. 'My mother, she's a Geisha. She ordered me to do a day at the Okiya... It really isn't nice! So after she let me go, I ran home, got changed into this and came here!'

'Okiya?'

'Geishas in training or where a few Geishas live before getting a Danna. In the Okiya mother works at, the eldest Geisha has no Danna! My mother is 30, getting ready for her so-called quote, unquote, graduation.' I looked at her intrigued. 'Have you ever read or watched *Memoirs of a Geisha* by Arthur Golden?'

'No, don't believe I have!' I said, smiling.

'Oh. My. GOD!' She dug into her bag and bought out an unread copy of the book. 'Read this. Long story short, it is about the most famous Geisha of all time and says about Okiyas! Mum is in the Okiya that it is set in. You need to read it.'

'Thank you! Are you sure, Toyoko?'

'I have so many copies at home. Keep it!' I smiled and hugged her. 'Anyways! Wish to get a drink and food?'

'Drink, yes, food, I just had some!'

'Fair enough! I know JUST the place! Follow me!' Toyoko said very excitedly as she grabbed my hand and ran towards an alleyway.

***

Toyoko lead me to a small little restaurant teahouse. 'I used to work here. On-the-house drinks still for me and you! Come on!' We walked in as I looked around. It was like a circus tent! Small on the outside, but on the inside, man, I shit you not, it felt bigger than my house at home! 'Two Saké!' The bartender smiled and waved at Toyoko who waved back.

'What is Saké?' I asked her in a slight horror of what I was going to be drinking.

'Fermented rice wine.' She sat me down at a table and sat opposite me. 'Don't worry! It is fresh Saké! Not Koshu! Not a fan of Koshu!' I looked at her confused like a pug does when its eyes open up wide. 'Basically it is a rougher version of Saké! Not as nice.'

'Oh.' The Saké was delivered in a bottle then two small little bowls. 'And yes, I can hold my drink. I can drink my father's under the table.'

'Good. I don't do that traditional stuff! DOWN THE HATCH!' I smiled and winked as I downed the whole bowl in one mouthful. 'How the—how the hell did you do that, Johnny?!'

'As I said I drink my fathers under the table,' I smiled as she tried to match me. 'Nah. Not as good, Toyoko! Anyways. Tell me a bit about yourself.' She poured herself and I some more Saké as I smiled.

'Well, Mr down-the-saké-in-one-go! I'm Toyoko, but you know that. Everyone calls me Yoko, which you can, you know about my mother too! Nothing much else really. And you?' We both sipped the Saké before laughing slightly.

'Well… I'm a father of two, my dads are gayer than pink farts and I co-own a company with my fathers in the UK, but we have come here, to lovely Kyoto, Japan to expand the company to here!'

'That is, actually very interesting!'

'How is your English so perfect? Down the the L's! Now THAT is interesting.' I asked her, very intrigued. 'I know it's a struggle for the Japanese.'

'It was a lesson of mine in school.'

'Ah!' I had the rest of my Saké and smiled again. *There's something special about her…* I thought to myself. *What would Eleanora think of me taking Toyoko in…?*

***

'Eleanora?' I asked as I crawled into bed at 11 pm exactly. 'Ah okay.' I put my arm around her and kissed her neck. She snuggled to me. 'She's asleep…' I stroked my hair and smiled. 'Good night, love.'

***

'Toyoko?' I called out the very next year.

'OVER HERE!' I heard Toyoko's small, little Japanese voice say. I saw her lying there again, under the blossoms. We were the only ones around. 'Hey Johnny!' She got up and hugged me.

'Hey, Toyoko!'

***

Dear Diary
Toyoko and I have hit it off! No one knows though…

Johnny

***

Chapter 9
Toyokō POV

I waited in the Okiya for my mother to hear news about my Mizuage. If you have read *Memoirs of a Geisha*, you will know what it is. But, if not, well, it's where a man's "eel" finds a "cave" he likes to live in. Basically, there is a bidding for a man to take the virginity of a Geisha... 'Komaki!' I heard my mother say. I walked in and bowed. 'Komaki. Get up and sit with us and your older sister.'

'Mother. Fukuchō.' I bowed to both and smiled. Nervously, I got up and sat down in between my mother and Fukuchō. 'Any news?'

'Sir Vaughn-Ray has won the bidding. A Johnathan Vaughn-ray.' I smiled as Fukuchō told me the great news. 'At 30,000¥.'

'Oh... Wow...' I said as I clasped my hands over my mouth in shock. 'That... What?'

'He has also proposed to be your Danna for a higher price of a further 300,000¥,' Mother replied. 'Making you, the most expensive Geisha in Kyoto.' I looked at my mother and older sister in even more shock than before. 'Your Mizuage will be next month. Become prepared, Komaki. You will be the head money maker.'

***

I stepped out into the room and saw Johnny sat on a freshly made futon. 'Are you okay, Toyoko?' I nodded. 'I won't hurt you, Toyoko.'

'Okay...' I breathed in as he turned around to go to the balcony.

'Saké? To calm your nerves.' I nodded as he poured Saké for me and himself. I walked on to the balcony and smiled at Johnny who looked as calm as ever. 'Toyoko... I have become your Danna for a reason.'

'What reason is that, Johnny?'

'You're coming to England with me.'

***

After the Mizuage took place, we laid there on the futon, breathing heavily. Not wanting to do a thing. 'You okay?' Johnny asked me amongst his heavy breath.

'I'm fine... It just hurts...' I looked to him, worried.

'That is normal, Toyoko... Come snuggle.' I shuffled up to him as I hugged him. 'It's all normal. You ready for England?'

'Yes...' I said, stifling a yawn.

'Sleep, Toyoko... You need it.'

***

Dear Diary

So glad Eleanora is on my side about this... I couldn't stand to see her go through this. Her mum has put her up to it! Oh well. I will be meeting her tomorrow. Ready to meet her mother and elder sister as Toyoko's Danna. This should be fun. Not. Oh well. It will be worth it to see her. But, the ceremony is next month. The meeting is to arrange said meeting. Facepalming so hard right now. I cannot use chopsticks for shit! Best learn quick! Don't wish to look like a fool.

Anyways. I best sleep.
Good night.

Johnny

***

Chapter 10
Toyoko POV

The ceremony was quick... Johnny is my *Danna*! Wow... And I am going to England?! A Geisha! In ENGLAND! He gave me an iPod before the flight, well, a few days before, it's cool! We were never really allowed things like this in the Okiya. The most we were allowed was a magazine to do with Geisha or the odd book! But this, this is amazing! He even got me something called Facebook! Also, what's a selfie? Oh well! It is such a cool, fascinating little piece of technology! What will be next! I know the flight is this morning. I can't sleep... I'm sneaking away... not fun. But worth it! His wife supports this though! Which is very good. Unusual for a sir's wife to support it... bless her. One day, I will be living with him... but I cannot talk English... I only know limited English as I was taught very oddly. If I had to refer to someone's wife, we were taught to say "Sirs Wife". That is about as much as I remember but I shall learn more soon! Who can help me with the English language? I know! it's (sorry) he's been in front of me the whole time! My "father-in-law" (he is my father-in-law due to Johnny being my Danna), George! Who else knows everything, or so he thinks! but, do I trust him? Do I trust him to give me the right information without any wind ups, that may I add he is very well known for? I cannot be seen to disgrace my family or homeland of japan after all! Bedtime... Goodnight.

***

Dear Diary

We landed in England, and Toyoko was just amazed and curious by England's ways. She asked if we can do anything here. 'Within reason. But no murdering, carrying a weapon and that here. Sorry, Toyoko.' She smiled and said that's fine. Then she asked, 'What about eating and walking at the same time?' I remember looking at her weirdly and nodding saying, 'Yes, you can…' then laughing.

Anyways… I best get to bed. Eleanora is asleep.

Good night.

The Immortality of Life

Dear Diary

My sons older than I am… Is that weird?

I'm 21 still, he's 30… What is going on? I have no idea… We still celebrate my birthday and death day. But I don't like this at all. I prefer being older than my son. Haha! But oh well… As my grandma would've said, 'You're shooting yourself up the ass with the sulking. Stop it.'

I told her about the fountain and she did the same as Steyvan and I… All of us are immortal… Just stuck in time of when we died.

***

Chapter 1
George POV

'Madre… What's wrong?' I said, hugging my mother who was in tears. 'Hey… Calm down…'

'It's a long story… I want to talk to Dad…' she said with a male-sounding, thick, Spanish accent. 'Can you call him please?'

'Sure… Just relax, okay?' I went out to the tannoy and pressed the button. 'Tim to Garcia's office. Tim to Garcia's office.' I went back into my office and sat down in my office chair. 'You okay, Johnny boy?'

'I'm good, Dad, thanks. You?'

'I'm good… Just organising the wedding,' I smiled. 'It's gonna be good! But, she has no one to give her away…'

'I would but I'm your family.' He sighed annoyed. 'Try Ash. He's a professional giver-awayer.'

'That's not a word, Dad.'

'It is now. Gonna go for a drive.' I grabbed the keys to my normal Lamborghini that I use. 'See you later…'

***

Dear Diary

No idea why Mum's so upset.
Bless her.
Anyways. Gonna go out with Steyvan, Johnny and Maz.
Bye!

Georgie xx

***

Chapter 2
George POV

I sat down after doing my makeup in an interviewer's chair opposite a blonde female ready to interview me. 'Hello Anolin!'

'Hallo, Melody,' I said, chuckling.

'So are you ready?' I nodded. 'Start rolling.' The people behind the cameras put thumbs up once they were all rolling. 'Hello Germany! I am here with our very own Anolin Vaughn-Ray. Anolin is George Lunar Vaughn-Ray's great grandson. So, Anolin, you look so much like George!'

'Haha, thank you. You look stunning as always, Melody! I have had a LOT of experience of doing his makeup,' I smiled and wave to the camera. 'Hey guys!'

'That is awesome! So now you are the new owner of your great grandfather's company. How is that fairing for you? I know it is hard enough just running a company on your own! But your great grandfathers?!'

'Well, I'm okay at the moment. I have my mother, Maribella, keeping an eye out.' I took a drink out of my flask next to me. 'But all is going well. We are having a memorial, again for him. But we are all doing well.'

'That is great to hear!' All of a sudden, my puppy leapt up on my knee and sat on my lap. 'Oh, hello! Who is this little pugalicious cutie?!' Melody exclaimed.

'Faun. My pug,' I said, smiling. 'Hello Faun! His name is really ironic as it's a black pug and the Siamese cat face marking pug is called a Faun pug.' Melody and I started laughing. 'Anyways… Sorry Faun! I'm a bit busy!'

'Anyways! Thank you, Anolin!'

'Thank you, Melody,' I said with a smile. While Melody was finishing up the interview, I took a drink of the coffee next to me. 'This is hard.'

'I bet it is, George! Where's Rose and Steyvan?' Melody asked calmly.

'Steyvan's just literally next door and Rose isn't well, bless her.' She smiled and shrugged. 'Yeah, Rose has some… lady problems.'

'I feel her pain, George. I really do.'

'Yeah, after come around and I will let you see her.' She nodded as Steyvan sat down next to me and smiled. 'Oh, hello, Mr Muscle!'

'Hello, Mother Mothra!' He gently kissed my cheek. 'So ready for part two?' I nodded as Melody had a drink of her water. 'You sure that's not vodka, Mel?'

'Hello, Steyvan! It might as well be. I need it! Suffering with this man right here!' I playfully shot her the middle finger. 'Oh shut it. Steyvan, what's your alias?'

'Lars. Now. Let's do this!'

***

'Okay, we have had a few emails for truth or dare for you two!' Melody said to Steyvan and me as we looked at each other terrified. 'Okay, Anolin, this one's for you from Sven in Munich! "I dare you to take off all your makeup, and stay makeup-less for the rest of the interview." Do you take this or not?!'

'Can I leave eyeliner on?' She shook her head. 'Damn it. Okay.' She handed me my makeup remover and I started taking off my full-on Goth makeup. 'Sven, you are a bastard,' I said, pointing to the camera after taking it off. 'This okay?' I looked in the camera lens. 'This okay, Sven? Thanks,' I said with sarcasm.

'You look so different! Anyways! Lars! This one's for you! It is a truth from Lena. Is it true, Lars, that your father was with Anolin's father and had children together?' Melody asked, smiling.

'They did. That's the thing. That's how I and Anolin are so close. We've been brought up together in the same place, time and more. I mean, I am not one of them, but my sister, Clara is their child.'

'That… is actually really heart melting! Aw! Okay! Another for Anolin. It's a truth, then I have to ask you a dare straight after. But with Lars, after this, you get one dare, and one truth.'

'Why do I always get the most dares?!' I asked, laughing. I picked up my drink and smiled a non-black-lipstick cheeky look.

''Cause you are the idiot,' Steyvan said to me trying not to laugh as I spat out my drink.

'Okay, you ready, Anolin?' I nodded. 'Is it true that you, Anolin and Lars are going out?' I nodded and took a sip of my drink. 'AW!' Melody exclaimed. 'Now, the dare. Here is a dare from Amelie from France! She dares you to streak around the company. Do you take this dare?' I took off my clothes and smiled. Melody giggled away and smiled. 'I take that as a yes! I think we need to censor this!'

***

'Don't get me started!' Steyvan said, laughing.

'Well, sadly boys, that's all we have time for!' Melody said to us with a sad tone.

'I'll say bye now. I need to get this out of my system! Bye, guys!' Steyvan said, going off set before blurting out in laughter.

'Goodbye, Lars! A huge thank you to Anolin and Lars for joining me today on set! And I hope to be joined by you two again very soon!' We both looked off the set to see Steyvan bent over laughing. 'And on that note, well, I should say laugh, Goodnight!'

'Bye everyone!' The cameras turned off as Melody smiled. 'That was pretty successful!'

'That it was, George! Hey, Steyvan... Have you got Rose's phone number?' I gave her my phone and smiled. 'I won't get any answer out of that for a while, will I?'

'Nope,' I replied bluntly. I downed the rest of my drink as Melody gave my phone back. 'Why did you want her number?'

'Well... I love her.' Melody said shyly.

'Aw! But... You do realise she will never age right, Mel?' I shook my shoulders to reveal my Black and White ombré wings again as Steyvan did the same.

'I know... I'm immortal too...'

***

'Rose? Someone is here to see you!' I called through to Steyvan's daughter.

'Okay...' I let Melody in and smiled.

'Ah bless.' I heard their talks while I sat in my office about the most random things and catch ups and more. It just made me smile. I went downstairs after a while in my office and hugged Steyvan from behind. 'Hello, sweetheart.'

'Heya, my Goth Moth.' He bent his head back and gave me a kiss. 'Come snuggle.' I jumped over the back of the sofa and snuggled up to my loving husband who was shirtless. I put my head into the nook of his shoulder and neck and my arm around him. 'You okay?'

'Yeah... Just... glad to have you back.' I wiped a tear away from my eye.

'What's up?' his English accent said, very concerned.

'Nothing... It's just... Those years without you were hell... Now you are back... It's like, my heart is whole again. Its beating with joy that you are back...' I replied smiling. I put my head on his chest and my hand on top of his heart. 'I've just missed your skin, your personality and more. I don't know what I would have done without you again, Steyvan.'

He started stroking my hair as I snuggled up more while he lay down on the sofa for the both of us to be comfier.

'Well. I'm here now… Just relax, my love. I will always be here.' I slowly fell asleep as he stroked my hair. The relaxing feeling of his hand just running through my hair and on my skin… It was the best thing ever felt…

***

Dear Diary

This has had to be the best night ever. He just hugged me till I fell asleep and I felt safe. I felt safe and happy. I didn't think about drugs, alcohol or relapsing or even self-harm at point. I felt good… Anyways. I'm going to go to bed. I need sleep.

Goodnight

George
Xxx

***

Chapter 3
Rose POV

'Rose... Someone's here to see you!' I heard George say through the door as I lay in bed with major pains.

'Okay...' I muttered. The door opened to see Melody walkthrough. 'MELODY?! OH MY GOD!' I sat up in bed and held out my arms for a hug. The door closed as Melody sat on the bed next to me and bear-hugged me. 'Okay. Okay. Mel. Period pains are happening!'

'Whoops! Sorry!' she let go and sighed. 'I missed you...'

'I missed you too...' I reached to my side and took some medication to help the pain. 'So, what you been up to?!'

'The normal! Interviewing, yada, yada, yada. Missing a good chat with you!' Melody smiled as we heard Dad's computer startup and then logic came up. 'Is he always like this?'

'Oh yeah, he'll go downstairs in a few,' I said, looking into Melody's eyes and looked at her blonde hair. 'You look stunning, Miss Halliwell,' I heard footsteps go downstairs as Melody sighed. 'You okay, Mel?'

'Um... Will you be my girlfriend?' I nodded and she sighed with relief and hugged me again.

'I will be! I can't go out tonight... Or I'd ask if you wanted to go for a drink...' she pulled out a bottle of wine out of her bag and a flask. 'Well then. Glasses are downstairs.'

'Okay. I'll be right back.' A few minutes later, she appeared with two glasses. 'I am always prepared. Even for a bit of fun.'

'Not this week, Mel! Just, pour the wine.' Melody laughed and poured the wine. 'Did you see Dad?' She handed me a glass as I took a sip.

'Both of them are dead to the world, snuggled up, I had to climb on the counter to get these and they didn't even wake up!' I laughed and smiled as we both took another sip. 'Want me to keep you company tonight?'

***

The next morning came around, I woke up with an empty bottle and two wine glasses on my bedside table and an arm around me. I saw Dad poke his head around the door and smile. I got up and plodded to the bathroom to change and clean the diva cup I had in, put it back in and then plodded back to get into bed. 'Morning, Mel…'

'Good morning… How you feeling?' Melody asked me with a very tired look.

'I'm good… Thanks for keeping me company.' I saw Dad cupping two hot chocolate in his hands, no makeup on, just a simple bare face and some pyjamas, stood at my door. 'Dad, you okay?'

'Thought you two would like these…' he said with his German accent as he handed Melody and me the cups. 'Your dad and I are going out, so don't throw a party while I'm gone.'

'Thanks… And we won't… Just a film I think,' I smiled and hugged Melody.

'Just Netflix and chill,' Melody said, making us laugh. 'Joking.'

'Good. See you girls later.' Dad closed my door and walked away as I heard him call out for my other dad.

'You okay, Mel?' She nodded. 'Good… Want to go out for a cuppa when my meds and that have kicked in?'

'Sure!'

***

Dear Diary

So glad Rose has found love. She's deserved it!

Died of hereditary cancer, came back through that fountain and still earned her wings.

She's been a doll and she's had a lot going on, yet… she's still helping. She's helping Steyvan and me with everything going on. Bless her.

Talking of Steyvan, he said he'll do a dear diary! He's never had a chance to write. There again… he doesn't. Lazy ass! But he's my lazy ass.

Talk later.

George!

***

Chapter 4
Steyvan POV

Okay. So, let's see if I can do this! I'm not much of a writing person. So, if it looks like shit, it probably is a bunch of shit. Probably me waffling on about why purple wears tinfoil hats to count pigs that are blue.

Let's try this!

Dear Diary

(At this point I've already given up. Until half hour later.) My life has been somewhat, messy, shall we say. I've been dead for over 100 years. But, everything still seems the same... I don't know if I am in limbo or what? I just feel happy though. Like I'm meant to be. I am with my love. George and he is with child... A little angelic girl... I'm going to be a father to an angelic, giggly little girl. Sorry, I can be a right soppy chop at times. Not usually like this!

Haha! Sorry about that! Um... what can I tell you? Well, then. I'm 127 years old (well, I still technically am 27!), I'm a dad, a bassist, a company owner... Well, I guess you know that. Oh. And a professional knob bucket.

When I died of testicular cancer, I never thought I'd see George for ages again. It was not ages exactly. But long enough. When I saw the black feathers and no one freaking out—I wondered what the hell was happening. Turns out, it was just George with his ombré wings! They still look divine! They are invisible to the human eye—but to us angels, we can still see them. We just have to remember to NOT float about around humans, haha! The family—Johnny etc.—it's okay, they know. But damn, we would be in so much freaking trouble if we did it in front of everyone else! Though… it would make for a cool gig (Note to self—bring that up to George).

With how we have been with each other, in life and death, it has amazed me how much love we have between each other. He has the face of an angel without makeup or with makeup and he's had a lot of thanks for me for helping and I to him… He… He has helped me through the hard times I've had with my life and he was there, right by my bedside holding my hand when I said my last goodbye… It was horrific for me. I couldn't breathe, it took over my lungs and my whole body… It was hard… I could barely get out "I love you". So glad I did though. Or I would not have forgiven myself to be honest.

Um… Now on a good—it's nearly Christmas! God, if I have to listen to Boney fucking M one more time, I will commit suicide. Okay, I'll live. But I won't live for that moment it's on the fucking TV. IT IS OVERPLAYED! Band Aid 1984 rescues it!

Anyways… It's George's birthday soon! What can I get a man that has everything? maybe some more black lipstick? or new platform boots? no idea! but, he shall be 150 Years old (we are immortal but we dont age in looks), but still looks 27… nothing can change my love for him. He's my angel… Literally. I would. Oh. Wait! I do! Damn that sexy peachy ass! STEYVAN, this is unlike you! But it's true! That ass! It's a nice ass! A German, Gothic, nice, sexy ass! Sorry.

Anyways. GOOD GOD, I NEED A PISS! Sorry… I just… am having a midlife crisis! I am 127! Leave me alone. Don't judge. I still look hot! I workout everyday, workout my wings and muscles (Hey girls! I'm not available! I'm way too old for you).

Well, I thought I'd share a poem with you that I've written… It's a bit shit. So sorry.

I first met you at the event
My heart was totally spent
That smile of jet black
Feelings you did not lack

You spoke to me so sweetly
And your looks so neatly
Your looks so Gothic
My love for you is chronic

God that was shit... So sorry you had to witness that. Just so sorry, haha.
Time to go!
Good night

Steyvan

Chapter 5
Steyvan POV

'OH, STEYVIE WEVIE, MY BABYWABY!' I heard my mother's voice ring out.

'George. Hide me,' I begged him as I heard Mum yell my nickname as a kid. 'Now.' George shoved me under the bed and flipped the blanket to where no one could see me.

'Hello, Mrs Vaughn-Ray.' I heard George say as his feet dangled off the bed. 'Stevyan's not here actually, he has gone to run errands. Sorry about that,' his German accent rung out nervously.

'When will he be back, George?'

'Sometime around lunch… He left quite early…' She nodded. 'Yes… he's doing me a few favours.'

'Fair enough. Had a fun night?' I nodded. 'Good…'

'Can I, um… Please. I'm kinda naked under this blanket… Couldn't wear any proper clothes last night… Hip was acting up.'

'Oh! Yep! Sorry! Is it okay if I can sit in the restaurant while I wait?' I nodded. 'Thank you!'

'Anytime, Caroline.' She left and closed the door. 'You're safe.'

'Thank you, sweetheart. Can't deal with that this morning!' George laughed as I came out from under the bed. 'Thank you for that lie too… She thinks I'm innocent.'

'That's bullshit. Anyways, I am going to get up, relax and then get on with stuff.'

'Okay, I'll be through soon, honey.' George got up and grabbed his clothes as his little butt wiggled, but it was perfect. A perfect view. 'Nice butt.' George laughed and flipped the finger.

'Fuck you,' George said with a sexy German accent.

'You did already,' I replied as George went into the bathroom. I lay back and relaxed in bed as George came out and crawled on top of me just after I pulled the blanket over me. 'Get to work.' I looked at his blacked-up face, clothes and hair that was in a bun. 'Love you…'

'Love you too…' George said right in my ear before kissing me. 'What's up?'

'Nothing… Just can't face Mum today!' I laughed as I slapped his butt. 'Get to work, you get some tonight. Tell Mum that I've been called to Germany or something.'

'Will do that for you. Love you, honey!' George got off and smiled. 'See you later.'

'Will do.' George shut the door as I rolled over onto my side.

***

'Steyvan…' I heard a gentle voice saying my name… female voice. 'Steyvan, wake up sweetie…'

'What…' I opened my eyes and rolled onto my back. 'Shit, sorry.' I rubbed my eyes to see my daughter looming over me. She was 24, bright white wings, blonde hair, with bright husky blue eyes. 'What's up, Rose?'

'Dad, it's 1pm… You've been asleep all day. Grandma has been asking where you are.'

'Shit… So sorry, Rose.' I sat up and relaxed in bed as she handed me a cup of coffee.

'Dad, it's fine… You must've needed it.' She sat next to me and smiled. 'Dad's keeping grandma entertained.' She smiled at me. 'So you might wanna get up.'

'Okay… Gimme 10 minutes.' I sat up and pointed to my chair by the window. 'Can you pass me my stuff? Need to at least make an effort to get dressed.' Rose threw over my stuff and flapped her wings to hit it over to me. 'That reflex?' She nodded.

'WING SLAP!' we said in unison while laughing.

'Come on, Dad, I'll help you.'

***

'Looking smart, Dad!' Rose said as I put on my "The Deathbeds" hoodie on. 'Ready?' I walked into the bathroom and looked at myself. White shirt, black ripped jeans and black hi-tops.

'Yep. I'm ready.'

'Good luck, Dad.'

'Thanks.' I walked out of my room and got greeted by George. 'So, she okay?'

'Yep… You might wanna run.'

'Oh God.' George nodded. 'Okay. Secret route?'

'Secret Route.' We ran outside of our bedroom. Until my worst nightmare was confirmed.

'OH, STEYVIE!'

'Oh God no…' I looked behind me and smiled. 'Hi, Mother. How are you?' I shivered so my wings would not be in her view.

'I'm fine! How were your errands?'

'Fine. Thanks, Mum.' I sighed and mouthed to George *"help me"*.

'Um, Caroline, do you mind if I knick Steyvan for a bit? It's to chat about the wedding and that lot,' George said, saving my ass.

'Sure,' my mother said as George and I walked into the bedroom.

'Thank you, George…' George closed the door and smiled at me. 'I just… Don't need it…' He put his arms around my waist and put his head on my forehead. 'Depression's hitting…' I shivered again and my wings came back as Georges ombré white and black wings wrapped around me.

'Steyvan… Do you want me to tell her not to bother you today?' I nodded. 'Okay… Give me a kiss…' I kissed him

173

lightly and put my forehead back onto his. 'I'll go tell her, sweetheart… Then well have a chat.'

'Okay…'

***

We lay in bed, in the stark, his wings over me for comfort and a huge smile on his face. 'So… What about the wedding chat?' I asked George.

'Well, that has been organised. So, do not worry. Meet me in the ballroom soon… Look smart… I have a surprise…' he replied to me, smiling.

'Okay…'

***

I did what George told me—look smart. I opted for a white suit and a black tie. I would've gone for grey, but white was the colour of the moment. 'Hmm… Prada or Gucci shoes?'

'Prada, Steyvan,' I heard a female voice behind me say. 'Gucci would just ruin it! Unless, you have any Louis Vuitton?' I turned around to see an old friend. Jessica, she was about 6 ft, brunette and adored her vintage clothing. She wore a pencil skirt in navy with buttons for decoration and a sweet pin-up sailor style top. 'No, not those! They are so last season! You got Beaubourg Derbys or Varenne Derbys, even Downtown Derbys?' I stood there with a pair of Gucci in my hands in shock. 'Okay. Let's get you sorted.'

'But… Jessica, you're dead…' I said in shock still.

'Hang on, no. My parents said that!' She walked over to my shoe rack and picked up my Varenne Derby shoes by Louis Vuitton. 'These with that suit.'

'Thanks…' I said to her, thinking. 'So… How's the child?'

'Fine. Misses his dad…' She sat me down on my bed and sat next to me. 'How's Rose?'

'The normal. Sex toys are in her room. She missed you too, Jessie. I did too… I know I'm gay as hell, but what happened? Jessie, I really missed you…' She put the shoes on the floor and hugged me. 'Jesus, sorry…' I sniffled a little and smiled.

'Well, they told you I died because they didn't want you seeing me anymore after I became pregnant…' I sighed quickly and looked at her confused. 'Now I am back. Here to support you and the family. I won't touch you though, I respect you and George. I also don't want him punching me in the head. Now, get those shoes on. I need your help. I am personally escorting you down to that ballroom.' She ruffled her ivory wings and smiled. 'Come on then!'

***

'So you know what's up?' I asked Jessica who was in the bathroom getting dressed.

'Yeah, and you best be on your best behaviour, young man! Your son is coming!' she said before opening the door. 'Bloody wings. Anyways, what do you think?'

'Lovely!' I said, standing up. 'Anyways… You ready?'

'Are you?' I nodded. 'Don't worry! It is nothing bad! Let's go!'

***

'Ready?' I nodded as she opened the doors to reveal the ballroom. 'Go get your Gothic angel.' I looked up to see black tourmaline, diamond and Selenite crystals. All shaped into sculptures of angels, and more.

'You what?'

***

I do